VANDAL CONFESSION

Vandal Confession

A Novel

Mitchell Gauvin

IN₁O₂IN₁
CANADA

*Publisher's note: This book is a work of fiction. Names, characters, places and
incidents are either the product of the author's imagination or are used
fictitiously, and any resemblance to actual persons living or dead
is entirely coincidental.*

Library and Archives Canada Cataloguing in Publication

Gauvin, Mitchell, 1989–, author
Vandal confession / Mitchell Gauvin.

ISBN 978–1–926942–97–1 (paperback)

I. Title.

PS8613.A9778V35 2015   C813'.6   C2015–904981–4

Printed and bound in Canada on 100% recycled paper.

Now Or Never Publishing
#313, 1255 Seymour Street
Vancouver, British Columbia
Canada V6B 0H1

nonpublishing.com
Fighting Words.

We gratefully acknowledge the support of the Canada Council for the Arts
and the British Columbia Arts Council for our publishing program.

For my Mom

"There is a tenderness in things. In things,
ruined. As if, freed from functions we bend
them to, they are newborn to the prime
unalphabeted world. As though this were possible."
~ Karen Solie, *The Vandal Confesses*

We're driving down a highway surrounded by evergreens in Felix's ugly blue Jaguar when the engine sputters and cuts out. This grandfather clock on four wheels lurches to a stop on an Ontario shoulder. A shoulder you wouldn't want to cry on.

I don't own a watch but I think it's around 10:00PM.

Felix and I were having a good chat about something before our chariot died and I can't remember what it was about, and now Felix won't say anything. He just turns the key in the ignition over and over again.

"It's not going to work," I say.

"Are you a mechanic?" Felix says.

"Do I look like a mechanic?"

"Dirty blue jeans and bargain bin sneakers unmatched with a checkered button shirt and a business jacket? You're right, you don't look like a mechanic. You're either homeless or the President of Iran," he says.

"Whatever, Gordon Gekko."

"God is my almighty dollar."

"It's not going to work," I say.

"I'm going to keep trying," Felix says.

I bet he can't remember if he put gas in the car or not. Every key turn brings him closer to the guilty realization.

"It's not the battery," he says, "radio still works."

I look out the back window down the two lane highway of darkness we've magically traversed, but see no splintering halos of oncoming traffic nor the devilish disks of red that shadow a car heading in the opposite direction. I look ahead in front of us and see the same canvas painted with black and dark shades of blue.

"You've ruined it," Felix says.

"What? The car?" I say.

"Did you fill it with gas?"

"Did I? You're looking at me? You're looking at blue jean George Bush on his Texas ranch. I don't even have a license."

"Now we're in the middle of fucking nowhere."

"We're still in Ontario, if that means anything."

I flip on a radio station for something to do, but Felix instantly switches it off.

"Do you want our battery to die as well?" he says.

"What do you want me to do?" I say. "Just check under the hood if you're so certain it still has gas."

"Wait, don't get out of the car," Felix says. "It's nighttime on a highway, you could get struck or eaten or something."

I get out of the car. The stones beneath my shoes part like the Red Sea and I nearly tumble into the highway ditch below. "It's perfectly safe," I say. "Pop the hood."

I hear the hood pop. Felix steps out of the car and rushes to the front.

"What portion of the country are you from where there's a threat of being eaten while your car is broken down?" I say.

"It's a scary place."

"No it isn't."

"Do you have a light?" Felix asks.

I pull out my cellphone, un-flip it. Felix flings open the hood and scans the metallic organs under lithium-powered blue light. He uselessly stares at the engine. I highlight particular tangles of pipe and wire as if I know what they do.

"Where are we, by the way?" I ask.

"I don't know," Felix says. "Do you think I should check the oil?"

"Sure, why not. How do you do that?"

Felix shrugs his shoulders, gazes out into the forest. "You don't think there's any animals hiding out there, do you? It doesn't look good to me."

"I think that's the thingy for checking the oil right there," I say, pointing to a silver stick jutting from the engine block.

"Aren't there bears or wolves out here?" he says.

"Actually that might be the anti-freeze."

"Statistics show moose are the most dangerous animal in Canada, not because they eat you but because they're just so big." he says. "We could get trampled if we stay here."

"Anti-freeze is blue, right?"

"There's also lynx, I think. Is it the lynx? Coyotes? Foxes? Eagles?"

"The engine is the only part of the car that can fail, right?" I say. "I mean, in terms of moving the car, obviously."

"You're the one dressed like a mechanic," he says.

"You should have dressed as a Park Ranger, maybe then you wouldn't be such a pussy about forest animals," I say.

"I don't want to be on this shoulder anymore, I'm closing the hood," he says. "Get back in the car, we'll have to call a tow trunk."

"Or we could just go get gas."

"Where?"

"I'm sure there's a house or something in either direction," I say. "One of us would have to stay with the car, though, which I vote to be me."

"We're not doing that."

"Cheaper than calling a tow truck."

"I don't care," he says.

Felix slams the hood shut, skirts back to the driver's side and steps in. I casually re-enter on the passenger's side. The smell of thirty-year-old wood trim and European cow leather stretched over metal seats is more poignant than I remember. It smells surgical.

"I'd go and get gas myself," I say, "but I'm not the one that forgot to fill up the tank in the first place."

"I didn't forget. It has gas," he says. "It won't work because it's a British-built piece of shit assembled out of old tin roofs in Sheffield or something."

"What is so scary about going to find gas?"

"It's not out of gas, moron," he says. "And I'm not scared, it's just dangerous."

"It's *not* dangerous," I say. "It's a Canadian forest; everything in there is more afraid of you than you are of it."

"That's bullshit. Have you ever heard of a bear having anthrophobia?" he says.

"Anthro what?"

"Exactly. A bear isn't afraid, it'll attack if it feels threatened."

"For the love of God," I say.

"If you think we're out of gas—and you would because you forgot to put it in—then go ahead, go find a home. I'll wait here," he says.

"It's not my responsibility to go find gas because it's not my fuckin' car and I didn't forget to put gas in it," I say.

Felix doesn't say anything. I scratch the wood trim and play with the glove compartment, flip through the owner's manual and rub my shoes on the car mat. If I were a kid right now, I'd be outside throwing stones, ruffling branches, playing in the ditch.

"Do you get service on your cellphone out here?" Felix says.

"Does a bear shit in the woods? And then senselessly attack car owners?" I say. "We're not in the middle of nowhere. I could reach the Pope if you really wanted to hear his sweet voice."

"Shut up and a call a tow truck."

I smack my phone into the palm of his hand. "By all means, the honour is yours," I say.

Felix stares at the phone for a couple of seconds, starts dialling well after the screen has gone into hibernation. The beeps and bops that spew from the phone's perforated plastic are somehow comforting in comparison to Felix's whining. He puts it to his ear.

The phone's ring cycle is interrupted rather quickly. "Hey honey, I'm just calling to say I'll be late," he says. "My car broke down on the way back into the city."

"Who the fuck?" I say.

"What? Oh no, it's just Xavier, he forgot to put gas in the car."

"No I fuckin' didn't. Who are you talking to?"

"I'll tell him he's a bitch for you, yes. I promise."

"You're an idiot."

"Okay, don't worry, I'll be back late tonight," he says, smiling brightly. "Love you too. See you soon. Bye."

Felix un–flips my phone and throws it back to me. "I had to make an important call."

"Calling your wife isn't an important call," I say.

"You wouldn't understand."

"I'm not calling the tow truck."

"Come on, man." Felix gestures for a fist bump, but I fail to reciprocate this universal symbol of brotherly love. I look out the window at the shaded trees and black ditch and continue playing with the car's interior, looking for warning labels to read.

"How *is* Sarah, by the way?" I ask.

"She's a bitch," Felix says.

"Nonsense, you hate women."

"No, I don't, honestly," he says. "Only her and at this particular moment."

"Why are you with her again?"

"She's a nice, genuine, honest, sweet person."

"Opposites do attract."

"But she's a control freak and a narcissist. It's like she has a split personality. Split between control freak and narcissist."

"Is that why you're so edgy?" I say.

"What do you mean? You mean apart from the fact my car's broken? Sarah's riding my ass about the employment thing," he says.

"Well, what does she do that's so special?"

"She's a . . ." he stops. "I want to say theatre director. She directs theatre, or a theatre directs her. She might work at a hot-dog stand for all I know."

"What you do isn't far off from what she does. It's only for less, that's all. Much, much, much less. Criminally less. Perhaps insanely less," I say.

"Yes, thank you. Don't remind me."

"You married her," I say, accusatory.

"Yes, and?" he says, defensively. "I wanted marriage. I value it. Like normal people."

"You mean like abnormal people," I say. "I have yet to find a person who gets married because they actually want it or enjoy it, as opposed to, you know, because their parents were married or because they don't have permission to fuck until God undoes their trousers."

"Marriage is the reason I exist."

"Not me. I'm a bastard child. Marriage is the reason why my parents divorced."

"At least I have a steady relationship. What do you have? A computer? Porn? Binoculars at the beach?"

"Escort services, my friend. And I'm not talking about a limousine ride."

"That's pretty cheap."

"Escort services are anything but cheap," I say. Felix shakes his head. "Don't give me your moral superiority crap, if I could find a person to stay with that I could boink every night, I'd be married too."

"I didn't marry Sarah for sex," he says.

"What? Why not?"

"What do you mean 'why not'? A healthy relationship is so much more than just pleasure. If life was just about sex we'd all be prostitutes."

"What a pity that would be."

"Are you going to call a tow truck?" Felix asks.

"Why should I? I don't have a wife waiting at home for me. I don't even have a cat waiting at home to be fed. I can wait here as long as need be," I say. "Hell, I'm even willing to sleep in the car until morning, when you finally grow a scrotum and go find gas."

Felix taps the glass panel encasing the car's various dials and indicators. He presses the reset button on the ticker that measures how many kilometres he's driven since he last reset it.

"Is there any other way of checking if it has fuel?" he says.

"I don't know, do you think there's a chance someone might have forgotten to put gas in the car?" I say.

"Don't worry, I forgive you. Blaming you won't get us back home, anyways."

"Prick."

"I heard you're writing a manuscript," he says.

"Don't change the subject. Your blame in this should be noted."

"I heard you're writing a manuscript," he repeats, "and need someone to read it over."

I reach to the backseat and pull out a stack of printed clipped packages from my bag. It warmly weighs in my lap, like the fickle, narcissistic cat a bachelor like myself should have in his single bedroom apartment.

"It's not finished," I say. "I sent a sample chapter to a publisher and they told me it needs more work."

"Let me help you," he says.

"I guess it couldn't hurt to get a good read through again."

"What's it about?"

"It's an autobiography," I say.

"About you?"

"No, about Napoleon," I say. "Of course it's about fuckin' me."

"But you're not famous," Felix says.

"I've had some unique experiences."

"Dipping chips in mayonnaise while watching pornography?"

"No."

"Dipping chips in whipped cream while watching re-runs of Seinfeld?"

"No!"

"How about that time your belt broke while watching that R-rated film in theatres, and you had to have your hand around your crotch to keep your pants up the entire time."

"None of those things are in here," I say.

"Well then it's not worth reading," he says.

"Just shut up and read it."

I throw him the stack; it thuds on his lap. He flips through the pages, seemingly calculating its length from its density.

"It's not very long," he says. "Aren't you a bit young to be writing an autobiography? We still have a good fifteen years before we can even have a legitimate mid-life crisis."

"And I'm excited for when that day comes," I say. "But I thought I'd get started on getting the last word."

"Your life is boring, though."

"It might be fucked up, but its not boring," I say. "Can you not see the marketing potential? Average nobody writes pure, honest portrayal of his fucked up life. The populist shit-eaters will eat this shit up. Gritty, dark accounts of bad parenting, worse fortune, sexual escapades, and symbolic drug use are totally in right now."

Felix repeats his inspection of the clipped pages by flipping through them over and over again. He hums and haws as he makes himself comfortable.

"I need you to do something for me," he says.

"Okay."

"Call a tow truck."

"What?"

"I'm doing you a favour by reading your manuscript," he says. "I'm actually trained as an editor and can request an hourly wage."

"You were the editor of a shitty high school newsletter and a second rate, unpopular partisan college pamphlet."

"Marx will be redeemed."

"Sure he will, and Jesus will walk among us again," I say. "I'm not calling a tow truck."

"I think you want to get home as much as I do," he says. "So I'll read your manuscript, but I'm going to leave you with the responsibility of calling a tow truck. In a couple of hours, either I'll be done reading this paper weight and we'll still be stuck here, closer to starvation, or I'll be done reading and a tow truck will conveniently leave us at our respective doorsteps just in time for me to hand back your professionally edited manuscript."

"You're blackmailing me," I say.

"No I'm not," he says. "For one thing, I'm not denying you the value of my professional editing skills."

"You mean high school level editing skills."

"Do you want me to read it or not?" he says. I let him continue. "I'm not blackmailing you, I'm leaving you with the decision to save us from certain peril."

"You're a moron."

"Why did you write it?" he asks. "Where did you get the time? The will? The support?"

"Your friendship is highly valued at this particular moment in time."

"Is this book going to contain nothing but insults towards the people you hate?"

"Would you be less inclined to read it if it did?" I say.

"I don't know if another clichéd rag of a story about your First World problems will appeal to people, as you sit in your perfectly lit home down the block from the coffee shop you complain about because a coffee costs fifty cents more. You know, in some parts of the world, walls count as a luxury," Felix says.

"My story is not cliché."

"What's your theme?"

I think for a minute. "My reconciliation with my own dissatisfaction."

"Too hard to swallow," he says. "Maybe I can help you rebrand the story so that it appeals to more demographics."

"Thank you for your input, Rebekah Brookes, but don't do that," I say. "I've already spent so much time compiling this mess there's no chance more editing is going to make it better."

I'm really beginning to feel the progression of one second following the other, the frustration wrought by knowing that each parcel of space-time is unfolding.

"How many times do you reference a cross-dressing pop diva?" Felix says.

I produce my out-of-date flip phone, flip it open and stop just as I'm about to dial. Felix doesn't take a glance. He shifts in his seat, looking for a snug position. "Let me tell you something about parents," I say.

"No."

"Parents come in four categories, and only one of those is good," I say. "And not many people get to see that category."

"Go write a self-help book if you're feeling morally righteous."

"The other three categories are ignorant, authoritative, and far-sighted," I explain. "Ignorant parents are obviously the ones that don't know what the hell they're doing. Authoritative parents are the ones that want control because after being pushed around as children they feel it's now their natural due to have children so they can be authoritative pricks. Finally, far-sighted parents are parents who have children to ensure people will be at their funerals."

Felix nods awkwardly and looks up at me. "Well?" he said.

"Well what?"

"Call the tow truck."

"Start reading then," I say.

We stare at each other suspiciously, on edge, waiting for a move. I dial. He starts reading. The phone begins to ring.

"Title Pending," Felix reads. "By Xavier Bernard. Crap title, crap story."

"Just read," I say, pointing sternly. Someone answers on the other end of my ringing phone. "Hello?" I say. "Is this . . . is this Maddog's Bulldog Pound, Break-down Service, and Flower Shop?"

"Yes, it is," the man says, his rough voice made worse by thick static. "Twenty-four hour service. Would you like to celebrate the coming of spring with some beautiful new geraniums? Limited time offer, they're ever so pretty."

"No, thank you, Maddog."

"Oh, I'm not Maddog."

"To whom am I speaking then?" I ask. "Mr. Flower Power perhaps?"

"I'm Maddog's nephew, Gravedigger."

"That's not your real name."

"I legally changed it."

"Why?"

"I have a role to play."

"Sounds like a pretty stupid reason to me."

"Excuse me?"

"Nothing."

"Sir, this is a busy business we run here," Gravedigger says. "Do you want to order some geraniums or not?"

"What? No, I need a tow truck."

"We do that too," he says. "Just tell me your location and the problem."

"My friends shitty Jaguar stalled," I say. "You see, my friend is from Buffalo so he's a bit thick and forgot to put gas in it."

"I'm not from Buffalo," Felix says.

"Out of gas? Where are you? There's probably some homes in the area or something that could help you with a bit of gas," Gravedigger says. "It'd be a whole lot simpler for all of us."

"Right. Unfortunately we're—according to my friend here—in one of the big African cat infested portions of Ontario. Perhaps we've stalled in a zoo."

"Excuse me?"

"So when can we expect you?" I sigh.

"Where are you again?"

"On one of the highways south of cottage country."

"What? That's in the middle of nowhere."

"So when can we expect you?"

"Well, my good sir, we're pretty busy picking up drunks closer to the city centre," Gravedigger explains, "so we'll be there in one, maybe two hours."

"Fine, whatever, we just need a tow truck."

"Would you like us to bring you some discounted geraniums? Half price for anyone who orders a tow truck."

I hang up.

"So he's coming, right?"

"Are you still reading?" I point to the manuscript in his lap.

"Yes, but what is this." He shows me a loose piece of paper tucked into the manuscript.

Dear Mr. Xavier Bernard,

We rejected your work due to the manuscript having numerous issues. Your obsession with sending our office a non-stop invasion of mail is what prompted this lengthy rejection letter. Let this be the final straw before we call the proper authorities. We had thought it would be obvious our responses (or lack thereof) would convey our disinterest in your work. But it would appear not, so please take note of the following sentiments:

We find this faux gritty, "down-to-earth" story a lame attempt to draw out false emotion. It seems you are trying to chronicle your life story as evinced by the highly emphasized "non-fiction" label plastered on the cover page. However, unless you always had a tape recorder handy, how did you memorize all that dialogue (of which there was entirely too much)? No one wants to read detailed descriptions of the mundane daily events of your entire life. We also found your use of both present and past tenses confusing. Are you looking back or are you reliving the experience?

On to the overbearing prose: George Orwell said that using everyday language in writing is best. We find it a pity you don't know this. Then there's the storyline. Where is it? Non-linearity, as you might have guessed, breaks flow, which is why so few actually use it, and why even fewer use it effectively. We have nothing against a well-fractured plot line. However, we usually publish writers who have done it with a reason and meaning in mind. You, on the other hand, seem to have done it for kicks. Further to this, not only is there no story, but the plot seems to be missing as well.

Above all, where is the passion, Mr. Bernard? Why would anyone want to read this? Your messy, unorganized and, frankly, boring story is a convoluted blurb of rhetoric without any clarity or coherence.

We wish you all the very best.

"I found this underneath the title page."

"I don't know," I sigh.

"Do they know it's an autobiography?" he asks. "What did you tell them?"

"I might not have labelled it that specifically."

Felix stares again, something he must do when he shifts his brain into mode. "How much of this book is real? I mean, how much actually happened?" he asks.

I shrug my shoulders, stall. "Most of it."

"Most of it?"

"Maybe."

"Maybe?"

"That's what I said," I say.

"That's what you said?"

"What does it matter? Read the damn thing already."

"When is the tow truck going to get here?" he asks.

"Don't worry, Gravedigger assured me that as soon as they finish chopping up their last customer they'll be here," I say. "Now, read!"

<Title Pending>

BY

Xavier Bernard

Chapter 1: Birth

Operator: This is 9-1-1, what is your emergency?

Caller: Um . . . yeah, my wife is pregnant.

Silence.

Operator: Okay. Is there an emergency, though?

Caller: I don't know, I think pregnancy seems like a pretty big emergency.

Operator: I understand. I don't think that's quite the sort of emergency a 9-1-1 response is appropriate for.

Caller: But what should I do?

Operator: About the pregnancy?

Caller: Yeah.

Operator: Well you have to wait nine months, for starters.

Caller: No. I mean, I know that.

From the background: Tell them I'm in labour!

Caller: Okay, okay, settle down. My wife is apparently in labour.

Operator: Uh . . . you mean to say she's about to give birth?

Caller: Yeah sure.

Operator: Then you need to take her to a hospital.

Caller: Can't.

Operator: Why not?

Caller: My car is broken. Fuckin' Dodge.

Operator: Okay.

Caller: That's why I'm calling you guys.

From the background: Do they need to know what I'm going to name him?

Caller: I'm taking care of it! We're not trying to pass through customs here.

From the background: Tell them I'm naming him Xavier.

Operator: Sir, are you in need of an ambulance?
Caller: Ma'am, I am in need of a lot more then that.

An ambulance eventually arrived and mother and father leapt in. Neither were really aware of what they had gotten themselves into. They could barely take care of a goldfish.

"Okay, ma'am, there's really nothing to worry about," said the medic. "Just try to breath regularly, we'll be there soon. Tell me if you feel uncomfortable at any point and I'll see what I can do."

"Is there anything you can prescribe?" she asked.

"Prescribe? Apart from breathing?"

"No I mean like medication?"

"You're pregnant. Additional medication might harm the child," the medic said.

"Fetus," father interrupted.

"You can't just prescribe me some prozac?" mother asked.

"Well, ma'am," the medic replied, "firstly, this is an ambulance. Secondly, we don't carry nor can we prescribe prozac. And thirdly, it's an anti-depressant."

"So no?"

"How about morphine?" father asked.

"Please, I understand both of you might be a little stressed over what's happening, but the best thing you can do for everyone's health is to relax," the medic said. "We'll be at the hospital soon."

"Can we go to that sick kids hospital?" father asked. "They have a Burger King near the emergency room."

The ambulance made its way to a hospital not of father's choosing. Mother was rushed to the labour ward while father looked for a cafeteria. In mother's hospital room, the doctor walked in.

"Hello Mrs. . . . Mrs. Bernard," the doctor said.

"Macshane," mother corrected.

"I'm sorry, Mrs. Macshane," the doctor said. "I'm Dr. Aider."

"I haven't taken my currently-off-looking-for-fast-food-stupid fiancé's last name yet," she said. "The wedding will be soon enough."

"I see."

"Still can't believe I said yes."

"Right, well you can certainly discuss that with your fiancé when he returns," the doctor said. "For now, I'm here to answer any questions you have as well as get some information on your medical history."

"That sounds good."

"First, do you have any questions?"

"Yes, is it too late to get an abortion? Or is that like supposed to happen later."

"Excuse me?" the doctor said.

"Is that a stupid question?"

"Do you know what an abortion is?"

"What are you talking about? I've had nine months to think about it," mother said.

"You can only have an abortion before a certain trimester, early on in the pregnancy when it's still considered a fetus and when its safe for you to undergo such an operation," he said.

"Oh I see. So it's for health reasons?" mother asked.

"There might be some ethical issues as well."

"That's unfortunate."

"Did you at any point discuss an abortion with your husband?" the doctor asked.

"Fiancé. He's been more worried about making sure Wheel of Fortune is taping at home."

"He's recording a game show while you're in labour?"

"I didn't like it at first, but he turned me onto it," mother said.

"I don't think that's legal, actually."

"What are you, my lawyer?"

Father walked in with a turkey sandwich in hand. "I was going to get you a ham sandwich, dear, but I couldn't remember if you were a vegetarian or not," he said, "so I got you a turkey club instead." He presented the sandwich.

"Turkey is a meat, brickhead," mother said.

"What? I thought vegetarian is the one where you can't eat pigs or shellfish."

"I think that's kosher," the doctor said.

"Oh, right," father replied. "Well, honey, aren't you kosher?"

"My family's Catholic, William," mother said.

"Really? Swear to God you said you were kosher."

"My family's been Catholic for four generations."

"I didn't even know Catholicism has been around for that long," father said. The buzz and beep of hospital equipment percolated above the ensuing silence.

"What should I do with the sandwich?" father asked at length.

"I can see you two need some bonding time," the doctor said, and headed for the doorway. "I can get this information later. For now, Ms. Macshane, I suggest trying to relax. I'll have a nurse come and check on you and help you prep."

"Prep for what?"

The doctor stopped. "The delivery," she said.

"Oh right, yes, sorry," mother replied. "I was thinking about the turkey sandwich."

The doctor sighed and headed out the doorway.

"Wait, honey, did you ask them about getting an abortion?" father asked.

"Yes!" the doctor yelled.

On mother's hospital television, through electrical witchcraft, a scratchy VCR tape transmitted old episodes of Wheel of Fortune in which three contestants fought to deduce phrases, buy symbols, and spin a brazen wheel that handed Lady Fortune a license to print and burn currency. A father of four from Tucson, Arizona guessed "Everything is better under the sun" when mother went into labour. Mother screamed and wailed as fortunes were won and lost. An army vet won a four-door sedan, a single cat lady guessed Michael Jackson, a Nevada computer technician settled for $5000, a hot single bachelor bought a vowel. And I was born nine episodes in, christened Xavier Rene Bernard.

Chapter 2: Home

Infant me was brought home to a little deformed house that stood unevenly alongside its deformed identical siblings and other infested apartment buildings on the border between Scarborough and Toronto. Built mid-century, our house was designed by amateur carpenters who looked at home construction as a do-it-yourself project for a summer weekend. Geometrically impossible doorways; hallways that caused psychological violence; rooms that couldn't fit more than a bed and dresser; shadows of a crucified Jesus staining every doorway, mementos from a previous owner.

Wooden and uneven overlapping sideboards masking poorly measured brickwork, an insipid white triangle hat, rectangular windows so small looking outside was akin to stargazing with a straw. The house had a crooked topographical footprint because one corner was closer to the sidewalk than the other. A house plotted sideways on a square plot of land.

Other anomalies took a finer eye: a screen door from a barn; front steps made from poorly sanded planks that let out a horrific scream and rattled with an eerie shake; blue paint peeling a little more every morning, whittling like a warped flower. The green pit of fake grass we called a lawn suffered ugly patches of yellow that dotted the ground like acne on a teenager's face. Dogs didn't care to shit on our lawn.

In some ways our disaster of a house was a blessing. If we had simply been suffering from aesthetic ineptitude, I would have done something myself about the stupid slant or the lethargic lawn when I was old enough to Fung Shui the place. The shabby construction, poor planning, and boring brick design ultimately helped us triumph against the municipal government with tax savings, an unheard of benefit of houses designed by drunks deliberating over department store catalogues. We saved money on property taxes because of some demented reason or mathematical inconsistency, or because our municipal politicians were also drunk, our house's slant took up less property than other homes did. I'm not aware of the exact amount we saved, but it was enough to justify remaining in the crap shack. Its small size also meant we paid less for heating during the winter and air conditioning during the summer. We also consumed less energy because of the insufficient number of electrical outlets—admittedly less an asset and more a problem given that on more than one occasion we needed to decide which was more essential, food or television.

Said crap shack—nicknamed Slanty McGee—stood inconveniently on a major one-way street that couldn't make up its mind as to which direction was the one way. Every now and then slack-jawed dullards with camcorders and camera cellphones gawked through cracked lens filters to enjoy the timeless classic we considered home, life, existence, etc.

Mother and father had bought the house on a whim just before I was born. Both were having trouble affording the respective bachelor pads they each owned, yet somehow combined they could afford a small suburban dwelling. They met in a diner one weekend, having dated for a while by then, and the discussion quickly turned to their future.

"Well, Debra," father said, "we can afford to either get married or find a place to live together."

"Those are our only two options?" mother asked.

"Well not exclusively. We could go on a cruise, but we'd have to live in a cardboard box."

"That's not what I meant."

"There's just no way to get both at the moment," he said.

"What about my mother and father, though," she said. "We're not supposed to be living together yet."

"Oh please, your family's Catholic, they can't be trusted," he said. "They object to us living together but say nothing about the fact we're having sex?"

"I don't pretend to understand their principles," she said. "In fact I don't even think they understand them themselves."

"But you care about what they think," he said.

"Because they're my parents," she said. "I don't really want to get married either, but it might be good security for both of us. What if we have a child or something."

"You can mark your calendar, neither of those things are going to happen."

"What about by accident?"

"What do you think is better for a child: its own room with two parents in a house, albeit unmarried, or a child sleeping between two bachelor pads?"

"I'm just considering the possibilities," mother said. "It doesn't matter if we don't want one, what matters is that it could happen, and I think we should be ready in case it does."

Father huffed.

"Maybe this is a good reason we shouldn't live together, let alone get married," mother said. "We clearly can't agree on how we want to live our lives."

"Wait, I'm sorry," father replied. "I'm just getting a little tense. We both live in pretty crappy places, we both need a new place to live, and I don't know about you but I have my heart set on being in the same wonderful house as the same wonderful person I love."

Mother huffed, rolled her eyes.

"I mean it," father said (he probably didn't), "but realistically we just don't have the money to afford both a house and your principles. Maybe some people can, but we can't."

They toured the only neighbourhood the real estate agent assumed was in range of what mother and father could afford. This initially involved condemned homes, crack houses, the dumpsters abutting crappy restaurants. Eventually they convinced the agent to move them up to something a little more liveable for human beings, but the fake border between the city of Toronto and the suburb of Scarborough wasn't exactly what they had in mind. The first and only house the agent would allow them into was none other then Slanty McGee. It had been on the market for nine months, and sat their waiting to devour a home buyer as the lawn of its front yard attempted to devour it. No one had maintained the house in the many months it sat empty. The previous owners had already vacated. I'm not sure what sort of lie the agent fed my parents, but it seems in retrospect too big to swallow. I can only imagine the agent left out a fair deal of the truth.

"It's a lovely street this particular fixer-upper is located on," the agent said. "Many beautiful modern homes in this part of the city. Amenities all very close."

"Tons of places to escape the house, eh?" father quipped.

"You could put it that way, yes," the agent replied.

"I see the previous owners weren't much into lawn care," mother said.

"You could put it that way, yes."

Even though the slanted sidewalk didn't prevent us from making it to the stairs or the door, there was, admittedly, a nagging feeling of inferiority. Something was wrong, not following the conformity of a perfectly symmetrical house. Sunlight peeked through the front window at an odd angle. North, East, South, and West were not linear with the placement of our couch, television, or other assorted crap. Something seemed wrong without parallel or perpendicular perceptions of cars passing by. We were on the map, but on the map at a slant. I couldn't complain. We could have lived in buildings designed around elevator shafts, shopping malls, convenience stores, mathematical algorithms. We could have lived in a place that only had purpose because of something else beside it. Slanty McGee was at least its own unique entity.

Stupid events managed to make our home a little less liveable over time. A transit bus, for instance, was once shoved by a cement truck into the corner of our house closest to the sidewalk. It was a spectacle, a temporary tourist trap. Befuddled engineers, more interested in cracking up over our crappy house, left the bus in its spot for days. The roof would collapse if they retrieved it. I had to wake up every morning to an atheistic bus ad proclaiming prophetically that there's probably no God and that I should stop worrying and get on with my life. I guess it's a sign of the times, the dead-end spiritual disputes reduced right before my eyes to a public transit advertisement.

In the end, engineers used the cement from the convicted cement truck to fill a foundation where the bus stood. The cement was going to dry within the truck's tube anyway and turn the entire thing into a Tonka-toy.

The eccentricities were piling up high by the time I reached the age of nine. On one rainy day, the back porch sank down to the ground as its foundation drowned in mud. The old birdbath in the back toppled and broke into many pieces, but for whatever reason those sickened little birds still used it. Some roof tiles blew off in wind speeds I could replicate with a ceiling fan. Our manual lawn mower hardened up in the crappy grass, rusted out, never to move again. Weeds crawled over it calling it their own.

There was nothing authentically beautiful about Slanty McGee—no hint of old Europe, immovable stone structures built on tradition, stone crosses with hearts of steel—just blue paint, planks of plastic and wood, and missing aesthetic essentials. There was something delicately immature about it, something tender. It was beautiful because it was home, because it was my ruined home.

We also had a knack for interior redecoration, but every time we moved the furniture around, put up more mementos or hung plants on the walls, nothing really changed. The interior was still defined by power bars and electrical outlets. There were still three bedrooms, one bathroom, and televisions in the living room, the kitchen and the master bedroom, all taking away much needed electrical outlets from lava lamps and dehumidifiers. Some dehumanizing commercial advert was always blaring on our white walls regardless of where the couch stood. Cracks in the ceiling from bathroom water damage were never fixed nor made less visible when the kitchen table was moved under them. The creak of a dry, rotten staircase never silenced itself. The banister was still loose even when polished. My window was still stuck even when cleaned or kicked in. We were never un-burglarized when we bought a new stereo and placed it exactly where the old one had once rattled. Old memories never returned when we put up framed photographs. Mother and Father were still weirdos, regardless of the art they hung, the food they ate, and the son they raised.

Slanty McGee served its purpose as my only childhood home, but there was no chance I'd remain with my parents when I was granted the gift of aesthetic purpose courtesy my own fantasies of shopping at IKEA. I was probably nineteen or twenty when I moved out. By then the mortgage on the house had been paid off, and I was the only thing holding mother and father hostage in the same home. Every now and again they'd ask if I was having any luck finding a new place to live, hoping the chain they were linked to through my presence was about to be broken. I'd give inconclusive answers to screw with them. I wanted to be just as unchained.

I got a job at Medieval Times tending the livestock like a chump circus employee, but I was a moderately well paid chump circus employee. I had the money and the job security but I had never lived anywhere else, so I called Felix for help.

Felix by then, with the help of his parents, had found a nice place of his own, a rented room in a house in the East End of Toronto. He shared it with a bunch of Christian frat boys he could Bible it up with. He had a girlfriend, a job, a life. Felix was set. He showed me around his neighbourhood and in no time we stumbled across a promising place, a 20-storey concrete block of an apartment building.

"Wow, what an ugly piece of shit this is," Felix said.

"Yeah but it's so cheap," I replied. "I can easily afford a room here."

"On your salary?"

"All encompassing," I said. "And by that I mean yes."

"It'd be nice to have you in the neighbourhood, but this doesn't look liveable."

"I have low standards when it comes to liveability," I said, "as long as it doesn't fall to pieces."

"Is it really that bad at your parent's place?" he asked.

"It's horrible," I said. "I mean I don't pay for rent, food or taxes, and I usually don't see them because we're all working now or they're at their friends' getting drunk—"

"Just the seventh circle of hell."

"But wait, I'm not finished," I continued. "They're annoying and selfish and passive-aggressive, and they watch weird television."

"But you don't have to pay for anything."

"I'm fine paying for things," I said, "it's just their presence I don't like. I know what they think, know what they'll do if I forget to do my dishes, or if they find me on the couch sleeping. They'll immediately think I'm lazy, not even pausing to ask if I've been working all day. They want to remain in their little pool of ignorance so they can convince themselves that kicking me out is an okay thing to do."

"Oh please, be real," he said. "This isn't Coronation Street."

We stepped into the building's foyer to take a gander, the usually locked lobby doors propped open. "My parents never did that to me," he continued. "Are you sure you aren't just seeing things or something?"

"It's a feeling," I said. "Let me put it this way. Your girlfriend, which one did you hook up with again?"

"Sarah. She's one of your best friends."

"Well, whatever, when you're around her, do you get that feeling that she likes you and that she wants to spend her time with you and make you happy?"

"Obviously."

"You can just tell. She doesn't have to say anything, its just a feeling you get," I said. "Well I get the exact opposite feeling from my parents."

"And you think everything is going to be better once you get away from them?"

"Doesn't matter how crappy of a place this is, it doesn't house my parents," I said. "That's all that matters."

Satellite images of the 20-storey concrete configuration showed a rigid trillium flower seared onto the Earth's topography. It was a broken thumb on a battered, disfigured hand. Miles of residences and rival homes surrounded this utilitarian delight, this mutilated madam circa 1960s madness. Its lax security originated from the idea that people were just too darn nice to break in and steal my stereo, stove, material soul. The building was built to degrade, grow old, grow uglier, and become little more than a bruise on the grid plan. To live in it was to return to tacky times, the timeless tradition of being forgotten.

When built, Whitey McConcrete proposed that living farther from the ground translated somehow as being worthy and unique. No one foresaw plumbing problems, flooding fountains, elevator malfunctions—the hamsters in their little wheels would go hungry. Commodious living was for the thrill seekers of greater affluence back when having abundant living space meant something. The hordes of parasitic poor people, however, wanted in as well. They too fell for the ideal of their own enclosed concrete skypods, their own slabs of balcony. I myself wanted to take showers above where water flows. The rich partook and then left, moving on to real luxuries like condominium ownership and mansions with heated car garages. The niche left over had its fillers, its sufferers, the forgotten few who, statistically speaking, were many.

The main foyer of Whitey McConcrete was bathed in cracked mirrors, broken candlesticks, hard lighting, and jagged limestone. The elevators were held up by shoestrings. Everything was yellow. In keeping with brevity, it was a fucking shithole, an embarrassing homage to society's inability to house every heap of homogenous onlooker, hoping that those who succumbed to such a dwelling didn't revolt against decade-old desire, lethargy, crap thinking.

Thanks to sparse parental donations, I rented a bachelor apartment on the seventh floor, but there's no love in a place you don't like, no hope in hopeless living. This was life in a hollow brick. I and my fellow apartment dwellers were the meat in a concrete sandwich. We were the rainbows in a void that accommodated only three colours: white, black, and dreary. Dreary became part of the spectrum, the crap spectrum. Living in that lifeless, lopsided, dilapidated lagoon of composites felt like a form of loneliness, a feeling of lost love. Living there reinforced that being alone was more than not having someone else around.

I wasn't some pompous stuck-up that couldn't live without continuous supplies of caviar or Cristal. I was adaptable, but there was a limit to the level of adaptation I could perform. My child-hood home was planked like a dog shed, but at least it was my dog shed, at least we could take it seriously as our home.

The concrete column I called my quarters was specifically constructed to disorient birds, povertize pigeons, and condemn the sun. It was put up ruined before it was even a residence. One couldn't consider oneself a full-fledged tax-paying citizen in that thing. We were just hungry hamsters humming bad music to out-of-tune harmonicas. We were the forgotten many.

My apartment, number something-or-rather, was a bachelor space, double the size of a shoebox. Appliances were archaic, assembled when society was still patriarchal: big steel monstrosi-ties with instruction manuals plastered with images of women. Every wall was white, simple paint plastered over pure concrete. A knock on the bottom floor vibrated to every other door. No sound was silenced, just muffled. Whitey McConcrete was really just one big un-insertable, un-pleasurable, invalid, misshapen, plas-tic, vibrating dick. Attractive and vulgar. The apartment was real-ly its own metaphor.

Despite being no bigger than two shoeboxes, my apartment had two bathrooms, presumably because engineers in the 60s thought generations would get progressively lazier. So inevitably such a misconceived invention suffered similar scars as Slanty McGee, thanks in no part to someone's entrenched sense of indi-vidualism. Instead of a broken-down manual lawnmower—hard-ened, mutilated, harbouring a new species of strangling weed—McConcrete boasted a fountain outside the front entrance, a.k.a. a coin pond, a.k.a. a pit of shit and garbage, a two-bit construc-tion job that went astray the minute someone thought fountains served a purpose apart from dirtying fresh water, drowning birds, idiot household pets, the lark. It was stained, scarred, and soaked—a slab of useless stone stuck in perfectly salient soil.

When I would wake up in the morning I would see the orange glow of the sun break through leafless trees highlighting the cracked pavement, the strewn leftovers of microwave meals, and angry motorists in tasteless forms of mobility. I felt like a for-gotten yawn of air. I felt like the blood-splattered body of a bug on someone's windshield, wiped off with carefully engineered wiper blades by some brooding businessman in a BMW.

I was once told that people who swear splice curse words into their sentences because they aren't smart enough to splice in real vocabulary. My homes were not spliced swears, pointless spaces filled in like bad vocabulary, engineers and faux-visionaries with too much time and money at their disposal. It was the way things turned out, simply put. Swears are the remnants of a ruined language, like the malleable yet immovable tenderness of a broken building. There's tenderness in things ruined.

Chapter 3: Family

When I was growing up, my mother and father took failed stabs at supplying a sense of normalcy. They stayed together despite no longer loving one another. They supplemented gestures of affection by requiring we have family dinner every night, followed by family channel surfing. They attempted to remain a unit. We went out once in a while like a big happy family to the movie theatre and the shopping malls. If it was a special night we'd fork over transit fare and head to the city's centre. I would see empty landscapes of advertisements, billboards, commercial propaganda, concrete, barren wastelands of malls, stores, parking lots, parking lamps, and restaurants every time I peered out the bus window. A wooden stage set held together with glue. Everything seemed slow, monotonous, and desolate. When the stores closed at night, the population of our bleak community went from thousands to a few janitors. It was a place made for people to be overcome by flashy lights that distracted visitors from the fact that they'd left a different version of reality a couple of kilometres back. I was confused at times as to why Mother and Father had chosen such a place in which to settle down. Mother hinted she didn't really like it. Father didn't care. Maybe it was the scarcity of churches in comparison to shopping malls.

William B. Bernard, my father, was born in Mont Blanc, France from a half-Algerian, cackling, fat carcass of a mother and a sly, slim, very French, self-obsessed father. When the fontanels of his head had barely been given enough time to close, his hot-headed parents moved to Halifax. Shortly after moving to Canada, father was blessed with a younger brother, Kurt Bernard.

Grandma and Grandpa Bernard were a mixed bag of goodies due to several continental crossings over the course of several generations. Cultural heritage to Father's family was better compared to a game of Jenga. Both were raised non-religious, but they mistook such doctrine as atheism in disguise and became leftist political trolls. After moving to Halifax, however, they became Christian slaves, cavalcading their ill-researched conservative values onto poor helpless Will. When Will was a teenager he rebelled, and as any reckless rebel would do, he returned to his entirely false roots. He started revelling in the splendours and spoils of atheism (which he hasn't looked back from since). Not at all caring for the actual doctrine, he simply wanted to strangle his parents' ad hoc beliefs. Of course his parents were proudly close-minded and wouldn't for a minute consider their son's anger, resentment, other emotional hoo-ha.

Will in adult form was barely a few inches taller than my height when I was nineteen. A plain face, plain spaghetti plate of hair as white as the driven snow, and as culturally cracked as a frozen lake. Without any real identity or trust in authority, it seemed natural he'd bloom into the cracked cast of atheism and conspiracy theory nut-job he is today. Yet Father Bernard rarely pandered to either, instead dallying in both in name only. Father once called the Canadian Mint "that organization that decides to put that stuck-up incest-producing imperialist on our money."

The brainless grandparents Bernard, after binding themselves to bland conservative values, also began, upon arrival, dressing like archetypal American Southern rednecks. They wore jerseys, worn out t-shirts, and baseball caps from crap sports that offered shit-all in the way of actual athletic competition, even though they had never crossed the 48th parallel. Grandma and Grandpa also at times wore the Confederate flag on some part of their clothing, clearly ill-informed of its history. Luckily for Mr. and Mrs. Dullard, the Maritimes seemed just as ill-informed. I guess it was understandable when they had white trash like Anne of Green Gables as an icon. Father Will, in response, dressed professionally at every opportunity. It was a mad dash to avoid his mad parents and their pervasive insult to American values that didn't exist.

So, in the end, my father grew up under shifting amounts of idiot authority; he went atheist and became a conspiracy theory nutcase minus the tinfoil hat, a bustling busy body with a Dodge Omni. He held doctrines he didn't believe in, kept books he never read, hung pictures he barely looked at. A mirror once shattered, but he didn't care. He just taped it up and put it back in the bathroom believing it was still good. Deep down, though, such a simpleton was quite complex, still a broken puzzle set of identities, cultural backgrounds, parental confusion, mistrust in authority and so on. Will did what anyone in his position would do to mediate curable wounds: he watched television.

He bought movies, television show box sets, and satellite entertainment packages. He circled dates for programs, those anticlimatic television "events" that magically sucked the importance out of life. His living room was a personal pharmacy of VHS tapes, floppy disks, rewinders, moving picture devices. He taped game shows and daytime television programs so he could watch them all when he got home from work.

He viewed himself as part of a misanthropic renaissance that found value in watching human beings humiliate themselves for ephemeral viewership, scepticism over the pursuit of scientific certainty, living room isolation on weekends over social outings. Father discovered this misanthropic philosophy in his teenage years while vandalising churches and participating in poorly attended anarchy riots. He soon found that the least amount of cognitive dissonance was achieved by avoiding contact with others. Family, marriage, friendship—these are futile social contracts performed out of an obsession for an unrealistic brand of normalcy. A healthy lifestyle is not dependent on positive thoughts, purity, proper relative relations, social contact, etc. Father lived it quite easily.

Mother was a similar story. She was an interesting figure from a family that only loved the members who agreed with the required family belief. Debra Macshane was Irish, or Scottish, or maybe English, or it could have been Welsh, perhaps from the Isle of Man? In some respects she was similar to Father and his family's Ferris wheel of pointless cultural backgrounds. Born in Barrie's Little Italy, littlest Debra was a rare Catholic "mistake."

Mother's family defeated the stereotype that Catholics just can't stop reproducing. She was an only child, and so her sin-fearing family's membership only tallied up to a mere three members. Despite generations of healthy worship, both on one continent and later in Little Italy, the threesome were "Catholically" asked not to continue attending church after it was discovered, horrifically, that Grandpa and Grandma Macshane dressed in white after Labour Day.

Mother was also a bastard child, and I recall that Father called her a bitch. She might have been that as well. Anyway, the Macshane Family Variety Hour, still very much vehement believers in their religion, were cast out of their church, doomed to practice and worship their God within their own private sphere. Mother matured to feel a sense of tragedy whenever she came across those Jesus-on-the-cross action figures nailed to the wall.

This personal revelation ushered in an era of Nihilist Catholicism for Debra, a deceptively simple de-emphasizing of Jesus or God as meaningful to spirituality, but still no less a part of a no less important non-sexual religious threesome. Mother said she believed in a "postmodern God," one that had no shortage of self-awareness or irony. I'm not exactly sure how that works out but whatever, it sounded cool.

This all turned out to be pointless. Mother eventually crucified her own ruined religious beliefs, the Nihilist aspect of her Catholicism being her guiding light. Grandpa and Grandma Macshane didn't even care to disown her upon her rejection of butchered Catholicism.

Debra in adult form had short, shoulder length, brunette-red hair and an unimpressive smile and frown. As white as the inside of a Golden Irish Potato, she on more than one occasion suffered an identity crisis, each occasion feeling edgy over being Irish or English or Scottish or Welsh or of any other sea salt drinking European lineage. Unlike Father and his family who weren't afraid to say "screw you" to the French, France, and half of Algeria, Mother cared to find a place for every one of her possible cultures.

On the other hand, tired of suffering from indecision, she didn't hesitate to divorce Will when she had the chance. I must have been eight or so. The unhappy couple, however, decided to stay "together" as divorcees within the slanted confines of Slanty McGee so they could raise their son "together." More importantly, though, the mortgage also needed to be paid off. *Then*, upon payment, could they truly split.

My parents in essence broke up the same way they had gotten together. Both times it centered on our home and the possibility of life, and how much life can cost. It's not clear why my parents did get divorced knowing they'd have to live in the same house for a little while longer. I guess they knew it was inevitable they'd split. All the reasons for splitting were old reasons, something intrinsic to who they each were well before they had ever met.

Halfway through my childhood, Slanty McGee took to housing my ruined family. Parent One and Parent Two slept in different rooms, forever fragmented by colourless drywall, though not thick enough to keep them from having sex. Staining the space above my doorway was the fuzzy shadow of a Jesus-on-the-cross action figure we could care less about.

During my torturous and tumultuous high school years, Mother and Father tactfully finished the rest of their separation, having remained legally married for roughly eight years. They made their separation socially legitimate, but remained in the same un-paid house. Their reasoning for staying together was that they loved me too much to go single-parent on my ass, knowing that children, teenagers, human pets are better raised under the roof of a house held up by two people's mutual hatred for one another, bonded together by a single lovable hinge (i.e. me).

Luckily for us, Slanty McGee was built as a three bedroom, so it allowed Mother and Father to live out their dream of having a successful divorce without the awkwardness of still sleeping in the same bed.

The same way you can't see my parents is strangely just the way I viewed my parents too. There was a mere tangential connectedness between them and the society they thought they were a part of. They were this reverse emboss effect of standing out in the wrong direction, yet they were perceived as being no different from anyone else. These were the little details, dots of distractions and dips in meaning that corrupted my view of what was otherwise a beautiful picture, a beautiful life.

It's my parents' fault, of course; they suffered from an endless yet eradicable parasite known as the "narcissism of minor differences." They engrained in me the value of suspicion (or is it irrationality?). Whatever it is, it's who I've become. Mother and Father protected me from everyone but themselves. They were the threat, the disease, and the cure. They're the snake whose bite will kill but whose venom serves as an antidote, and I've learned that what doesn't kill me will only make me more scared shitless of what will.

I only met Father's younger brother Kurt once, and I don't remember it well. Growing up, Kurt—by the only account I know—was a mischievous little shitmouse. From age five to age eighteen, he cared little for the Bernard family values. He stuffed snow into mailboxes, pulled apartment fire alarms, threw stones at speeding cars, kicked down road signs, stole socks from department stores. Kurt's low I.Q. was evenly matched by his unusual access to rational thinking. He could rationalize his way through a prank or practical joke, but he always failed at avoiding capture. His ability to reason kept him afloat but not out of trouble. Grandma and Grandpa Bernard were at a loss for solutions. Without any rational calculation left for themselves, they let Kurt be Kurt with a few ineffectual moments of "Stop that, you worthless little shit," or, upon his ascension to high school, "Stop that, you worthless shit." When Kurt dropped out of high school, Grandma and Grandpa Bernard had elevated their standards of thinking up to the 1950s, having previously been maintaining levels standard for 16th century peasants. Kurt was forced to sign up for the military to "straighten up."

Kurt, despite his mischief making, had grown up under a peculiar umbrella of parental protectionism. He had been emotionally harboured and, as a result, was a rather fragile human being, a less armoured descendent of Grandma and Grandpa Bernard's impeccable stupidity. Kurt enlisted not having anything better to do with his life. He was asked to keep a diary to record his time in training and possible combat. Here's his first entry:

> *Dear Diary . . .*
> *I hate writing diaries.*

That's also his only entry. Kurt spent four years in the military before quitting, returning as the hoped for, straightened up, strapping young man plastered across recruit posters and pamphlets. He welcomed himself back into private life by spending one night in his parents' home before breaking out of his basement room, disappearing for five days, and then admitting himself to a mental hospital.

Contact was closeted at best for the next couple of years. He divulged little in the way of anything, sending simple yet suspicious letters of his health and wellbeing.

Many, many months after that, if I'm following time correctly, Kurt spontaneously invited the immediate family to his new pad: a one bedroom apartment in a government housing project. His new job as Warehouse Manager for an appliance manufacturer was a glorious step towards mediocrity. Kurt was a rejuvenated success by any measure, a rehabilitated census statistic on the road towards complete consumption by conformity. The intense work of trained professionals had helped to ensure his mental and emotional problems wouldn't get in the way of his living life. But Kurt hadn't invited Grandma and Grandpa, Mother and Father, and me (still stuck at a one-digit age) over to his place to brag. We sat around his half-kitchen, half-living room combination, Kurt's bald head shining under bad lighting. He quieted us down and spoke solemnly: "It's nice to see you all."

"It's nice to see you, Kurt," Grandma said.

"I didn't invite you here for a family event. I have some weight still on my shoulders," he continued. He wasn't making a lot of eye contact. "Mom, Dad," he turned to the two, "I learned about forgiveness over the years and I've tried to do it myself. But it would help if you admitted you were bad parents."

Any person could rationalize that's not something you demand of your parents, especially of Grandma and Grandpa, who were not even smart enough to speak nonsense. Kurt, unfortunately, had spent much of his life ignoring others, especially his parents. Then again, Kurt didn't care. He had never cared. He had lived most of his life up to that point finding pleasure and peace in avoiding things others embraced. He never drank beer or smoked cigarettes. He refused party invitations and bar nights. On some occasions he would spend hours riding streetcars in Toronto, staying in the back as it looped around and laboriously returned to the station. He never let anyone's definition of fun or dignity get to his head. Kurt was very much what most wanted to be as well as what most wanted to avoid. I guess people found pleasure in that sort of contradiction. They cocooned themselves in criticism of Kurt's condition, whatever it was. The military had ruined a once perfectly ruined being. It had wrinkled the creases.

The tension in the room was palpable and strangely climatic. For much of the silence Grandma and Grandpa Bernard looked between themselves and Kurt, trying to read each other's thoughts (to no avail). Grandpa finally rose to his feet, a defiant look on his dreary face. "You worthless shit!" he grumbled loudly.

How nice of him to remember.

Kurt was unnerved. Father rolled his eyes.

"Kurt, we have no qualms about how we raised you or your brother and sister," he continued. "We didn't always have a lot of resources, I'll admit that, but your fucking attitude was a pain in the ass."

Kurt didn't blink. "I asked for a simple apology," he sighed, turning away.

Father finally rose. "Mother, Father; I think this is the best time to say that I agree with Kurt," he said. "You can't even see how bad you were at parenting."

"Oh, come on, you guys were terrible kids."

"That's beside the point!"

"We didn't even want to have children," Grandpa continued.

"If we were little shits growing up, guess whose fault that was," Father said.

"Show some respect, Will," Grandma butted in.

"For what exactly?" Father replied.

There was an eruption of chatter, a swirling whirlwind of spit and sayings, statements of innocence and pointless rhetoric. Within minutes we had all left, leaping out after labelling each other with stupid words.

Contact amongst family has remained sparse since then. Sometimes if a BBQ was being held, we would grudgingly converge in the same backyard, but discussion was meagre and minimal, filled with pointless questions and descriptions of lifeless activities or events. We were all just acquiescing, just people drinking beer, smoking cigarettes, worthless little shits.

Mother and Father made sure our fridge was stocked with alcohol. I'd come home from school, stumble into the kitchen in search of after school snakes, open up the fridge and find mysterious brown paper bags stuffed in the top shelf. The golden necks of glass beer bottles would be poking from the top. Mother and father would come home from work soon after, swerve into the kitchen, inanely open and close drawers, float around the counters for a while waiting for me to be out of sight before proclaiming a defeat at the hands of thirst and popping open a bottle of beer. They'd sooth their throats with the stuff whenever they could, and they turned to it so often supplies usually ran short. Within the hour of returning home—Father from his pseudo-managerial job at a photography outlet and Mother from whatever it was she did—they'd have a bottle in hand. If it was the weekend, they'd quench their thirst enough to spout some soggy thoughts, their brains floating in a layer of hops and water.

Shortly after I moved away from Slanty McGee into Whitey McConcrete, Dad had decided to drink down dozens of sample-sized alcohol teasers he had collected over the years. In the afternoon, I arrived at his place after he had called mine, his voice loud and floundering in a lazy flow of static through his cellphone. I knocked on his front door.

"Let's go for lunch," I said, holding his door wide open.

"That's what they expect us to do," he bumbled, standing as erect as a flag pole. It looked like he was having trouble keeping the pose.

"What?"

"It's conformist!"

"It's the afternoon."

"Exactly. Let's go later . . . really throw them off."

"Who's they?"

"They got you too, eh?" he smiled.

He was full of movie quotes and recanted scenes, mementos to simplified truths and rewritten familiar stories that were increasingly irrelevant. He thought he was speaking sincerely of sacred teachings and essential social lessons, but watching *Rambo* never taught anyone life lessons; watching *Wall Street* never taught anyone how to do business; although, watching *Crocodile Dundee* will teach you why no one likes the 1980s. One night, Father was mindlessly watching television with me enthralled in the experience beside him. I was somewhere between the ages of fourteen and nineteen, I'm sure of it. Mother was somewhere else. He said, "You know, son . . . boy, the meaning to life is," he struggled, "I'm . . . this . . . I'm sure this matters. The meaning to life is: there are seven levels."

To many clear thinking human beings, that doesn't make a shit of sense. It's just the talk of tipsiness. I, however, took Father's stumbling speech as a special case of unearthed inspiration. I nearly went mad trying to decode his meaning, the message behind the muttering.

I never did.

In fact, after much more of my father's talkative tipsiness, I grew tired of trying, realizing he was simply drunk—a damaged emoticon drinking to forget something previous. A number of numberless years later, I was absentmindedly viewing *The Beatles Anthology* documentary when Father's exact quote blared forth from Paul McCartney's Liverpool accent as he recounted an LSD trip, stinging me with its familiarity.

Father's wisdom was not always weak in logic. It was more of a slot machine. Most of the time it spewed moth balls, aged coins worth little. But once in a while, when things were ripe, gold was in flight.

Stumbling out of some bar late one night, me in my early twenties, Father trotting along like a race horse with three legs, we made our way to a public bus. I had downed two beers too quickly, so I was a little off my rocker myself. Father broke out with a batch of words. "Have you ever noticed," he bumbled, his eyes half shut, "if you take a big huge big green grass field . . . and you place hundreds of people in it walking in whichever direction . . . everyone looks directionless, everyone looks aimless, without purpose." He took a breath. "Yet take away all but one, but one, and suddenly that one person is human, has purpose, has direction . . . what . . . ha! . . . what is that?"

"People are hell," I spouted, ignoring him. "People are hell."

Mother at times would get in on the nuttery. If we were bored together or out of ideas we'd sit together as the glued together family we were meant to be and watch television, my parents keeping tabs on the amount of empty space in a beer bottle. As clichés clicked on the screen in front of us, Mother and Father would become their usual poetic selves.

"Rain is nothing but an excuse for umbrella combat," Mother gobbled.

"Shhh," Dad spat, "television . . . pay attention."

"I don't like *Wheel of Fortune*," I said.

"It's important."

"What's important? The television or what's on the television?"

"TV. Call it that, abbreviated."

"It's already abbreviated," I said.

Mother laughed.

"Why do drunks speak unrealistically?" I continued, annoyed.

"Oh, don't go there, will you?" Father said, angrily. "Show some respect. We're not drunks."

"Uh huh."

The whirl of a clickity wheel, the chants of a Los Angeles audience.

"There are three things I learned," Mother broke in.

"I'm going to bed," I said.

"What? It's only 7:30," she said. "Wait."

"What?"

"Let me tell you them," she began. "Everyone wants their opinion heard. Everyone wants to be told they're beautiful. Always say goodbye."

"You learned something everyone already knows," I said.

They stared.

"Goodbye," I waved, and went to bed.

Our family conversations were musings on television programming, discourse centered on the seeping sound of artificial noise coming from our living room. When I bolted forth from Slanty McGee to Whitey McConcrete, Mother and Father took the first opportunity to say good riddance to our crap shack and move out in their own separate directions. Father found a flat in an old converted fabric softener and household poison factory. The place smelled enchanted. Mother moved to an aged, spandrel decked condo—a two bedroom white-washed glass cube in one of those fancy condo communities, complete with all the frilly amenities, like a fitness centre overlooking a bank lobby. There were no gates or girders, just glass and curtains. Great price for a hamster cage—a hamster cage community.

Dad called the very next day. He had no qualms about his intentions. "Come over to my place and see what a man with real taste looks like," he said.

"Sounds homosexual."

"Shut up."

I took a taxi cab in light of the fact that I hate public transit. Too many memories from growing up on buses, streetcars, subways—riding them a choir of a pastime for a bored, hyperactive little freak like me. Mechanical babysitters for my parents and nothing else. Sometime when I was younger than ten, Father and I would find ourselves on a bus on more occasions than he would like to admit. He was adverse to taking transit as well, mainly because there were other people. He said it was the feel and the smell that bothered him, but he fooled no one.

One day, I found myself on a bus in a single seat with Father sitting behind, keeping an eye on me, because apparently transit riding incurs the same risks for children as does an overseas tour of duty. My left leg rested on a protruding silver baseboard heater, an unmoving metal log that clanked and wheezed every so often.

Staring out the window at the blurry forest of flesh, ferns, and concrete, I noticed there was a peculiar ping ringing through a tiresome crowd of faceless, nameless riders. I looked to the seat in front of me: another grey and red single seat, and in it, a balding, wrinkly old man with a dirty winter coat and a halo of white hair. Another solemn ping rang amongst a concoction of frozen sound—and then another. I peered down towards the baseboard heater. A handful of quarters, loonies, and toonies rattled atop the silver exterior. I gawked in confusion. The change was flowing out of the old man's pockets in front of me, unbeknownst to him. The wrinkly old puppet continued to bob up and down with the bus.

I was bewildered. I looked to Father. He had a subtle, crazed smile on his face as he too watched the plunking change. He had tunnel vision, it appeared. I tried to mutter a word, but Father broke in with a sturdy point of his finger and a hushed voice. "Go," he demanded. "Pick it up! Yes, get it."

I gleefully reached down and stole the old man's change, and as the rest emptied out of his pockets, I handed it too to my father behind me. I didn't care to see if others noticed or to doubt whether taking it was the right thing to do. I wonder what happened when the old man went to order a coffee, only to discover his dirty khaki pants no longer held any change. Was I the thief, or was my father?

Back in the taxi, the International Relations major driving me to father's flat explained the West's double standards on Somalia and the Darfur region of Sudan and how to bring peace to the Horn of Africa. Just as he was about to expand on his ideas on militias and tribalism, we hit some pompously chromed Escalade parked outside a bullet-proof mini-mart. The emblem had been reworked into a gang symbol. The taxi was not totalled. It was only a simple fender bender, the Escalade escaping with only an orange curve across its chrome. I paid the driver what I would have owed had we made it and started walking, getting to Dad's in minutes.

"Wow, you're here quick," he said, answering the door.

"I am?" I asked.

"Transit?"

"I took a cab—that hit a parked car."

"It was one of those poorly parked fucking gangster tanks, wasn't it?" he said. "Wouldn't those people save more money if they bought more economically?"

"I didn't ask."

"What?"

"Nothing."

Father's flat was fantastically adorned, trimmed with whatever caught his eye during random recons of the home décor aisle. He had splurged on shiny garbage cans, Wal-Mart art, various electronic devices. The television was powered on, producing flash after flash of light pollution, populations of primary colours merging into images of whatever people are willing to watch, which is always anything. Father was a bachelor to women, but a taken viewer to the market.

I had trouble knowing where to sit. I didn't want to touch anything. I found a beanbag chair beside his TV and sank in. Father sat down on his two-person love sofa, opposite some soap opera.

"What is this?" I said.

"What is what?"

"I'm sitting on a beanbag chair."

"I like it."

"Trying to relive your childhood, huh?"

"I didn't have a childhood," he said.

"Come again?" I asked. It seemed Father was binging on bad thoughts again.

"Childhood is supposed to be a time of innocence, when you are stupidly and blithely aware of nothing, which puts you pretty much one level above household pets," he said.

"And that's not what you had?"

"All I did growing up was hate my parents, trying to leave at every opportunity through useless proxies," Father continued.

"Did you buy a thesaurus?"

"I missed something. I've always had some sort of direction it seems."

"Pity," I said, unimpressed. "So you were born to hate your parents, is that what you're saying?"

He nodded and sighed with a heavy wheeze. "Have you talked to your mother yet?" he asked.

"No," I said.

"Still a bitch, I bet."

"That's nice of you. Send her an 'I think you're a bitch' Hallmark card. I think they just came out with them."

"What?"

"What do you mean what?" I said. "We're family, for Christ's sake, and you've been de-married for years—get over it."

"I'm allowed to hold on to a little resentment," Father said. "Just wait until you get married, you'll see."

"I can't wait," I said. "Sounds like paradise."

"You will, everyone usually does," Father said.

"Are you familiar with my generation?" I asked.

"I know it doesn't always seem like it, but marriage can be the greatest sign of someone's love and emotional maturity," he continued, "or at least it was once, but now its only purpose is to force two people who don't love one another into an awkward form of imprisonment that allows the government to charge exorbitant sums of money to simply leave one another. That's why when you get married, do it as a business choice. Marriage can be a financial benefit if you do it right. I did it wrong. Don't do what I did."

"You're kidding."

"What?"

"What about the love?" I asked.

"Oh there's no such thing," he said. "It's all just emotions. Don't listen to your emotions, listen to reason."

"So you're telling me I shouldn't listen to how I immediately experience the world?" I said. "Just calculate everything?"

"Where the fuck has love taken you recently, huh? That Lillie girl that left you or whatever? That fundamentalist Christian friend of yours that thinks God cares about how he uses his dick?"

"You work in a crummy photography office with jail bars over the windows."

"You live in a crummy apartment," he said.

"It was your married generation that made those concrete things."

"We had fun."

"You fucked things up is what you did. You guys got serious about shit all. Now I have to get serious about fixing it," I said.

"Hey, you're the cellphone culture, the cellular generation," he said.

"Oh, swell, and what did you guys do? Dirty a cow pasture?"

"What do you have against me and your mother?" Dad asked.

I paused, taken aback. "Nothing," I sighed.

CHAPTER 4: LOVE

Every afternoon I'd wake up, shit and shower, French press a coffee, boil a bowl of oats, and head off to work. I'd walk the length of the hallway towards the elevators hoping not to run into anyone. Neighbours were not people, they were weird noises in the walls, unexplained tremors in the floor, the freaks that pulled the fire alarm. If I heard the thud of footprints against the stained carpet, I'd wait to walk out my door until it was clear, even if I was late for work. On some days I wasn't so lucky. I'd be walking down the long hall and see someone's shadow fizzing under the fluorescent lights. I'd measure my pace, wishing I didn't have to round the corner. What monster would it be? A little old lady with a pushcart of laundry and an accent I couldn't comprehend?

One day, I was riding in the elevator down to the main floor having not seen a soul alive. The doors buzzed open. I quickly glanced at the cracked mirrors trying to foresee if awkward avoidance of eye contact would take place. I spied the warped dimensions of a ponytail, a female form waiting to ride the elevator I'd commandeered. I walked out of the poorly lit box and standing before the three elevators was a woman around my twenty-something age, her left hand on her hip, leaning slightly to the left, impatient. Reddish brunette hair, almost my height, small brown eyes, other random male value judgments, various fetishes and fantasies.

After that, I started taking pointless trips to the corner store and laundromat hoping to run into her again. For a week I couldn't find her. I'd run into the usual—the laconic bus driver, the old woman I couldn't understand, the redneck landlord, the pizza guy, the satellite installer—but never her.

Eventually, I found my chance. I found her waiting for the same elevator as I was.

"Fancy seeing you here," I said.

"I live here."

I paused. "I know, I mean . . ."

I looked her over, looking for details to notice, details I could question and start a conversation. I dotted across her body, picking apart pieces and paraphernalia that might hold meaning for her. She was no mystery or enigma, though. She was simply a biological complexity, a former fetus all grown up.

"So how do you like living in this apartment building?" I asked.

The elevator suddenly opened. She walked in and I followed. She pressed the button for penthouse.

"Penthouse?" I said. "Wow, you must be rich."

"To live here?" she replied.

"I mean it's a dump of a place, but still."

"What floor do you want?" she asked.

The elevator started to ascend. "One," I said.

She looked at me. She could see the false sense of pride developing within me.

"So how do you afford a penthouse?" I said.

"It's my parent's place," she said, watching the numbers. "My parents have been living here as long as I can remember."

"How long can you remember?"

"You just moved in didn't you?" she asked.

"Yeah I rent a place on the main level," I said. "How'd you know?"

"Because no one talks to each other here."

Had I violated a law? She was laughing at my befuddlement. The small dark eyes I had noticed on her before seemed like such a useless detail in the face of my naivety. So many useless details, so many pointless mathematical dimensions.

We arrived at her floor; she waived and stepped off. I rode the elevator back down alone to my own.

We ran into each other more often, learned more about each other, increased the length of our conversations each time we met. Her name was Lillie. We were on the same page somehow, we shared brain waves. We became girlfriend and boyfriend.

When Lillie got bored she seemed prone to becoming a spiritual nut-bar, someone who believed in the power of miracles, positive thoughts, prayer, therapeutic bath salts. She'd come home, light some incense, push play on the Pink Floyd CD, try to interpret tarot cards, look up discount palm readings on the back pages of a free newspaper. She'd watch bright and breezy news stories of sinking ships with surviving sailors and praise the coincidence of some religious blessing. By dinner time she'd be wrapped up in ensuring her own miraculous moment, anything to feel connected to an obscure spiritual force that didn't necessarily reciprocate the sort of good fortune she believed it would deliver.

While watching one local news team spill their guts over such a story, it turned out one blessedly sick kid was being housed and drugged up to his eyeballs in our very own city. Miracles apparently can happen locally. I didn't think Lillie would make anything of it. Never meet your heroes, right?

"Oh my God! Right here! Down the street!" she said. We were on the couch I had stolen from my dad.

"Could you play along here?" I asked, necking her. "I'm young. I'm also impatient."

"Stop it," she said, hitting me on the forehead. "This is important."

"What? The kid? Why do you think they showed it at the end of the broadcast?"

"They had to fit it in somewhere."

"Tomorrow is Sunday, which means tonight is Saturday, which means—"

"I know. But this is more important than sex."

"Everything is more important than sex," I said. "Everyone knows that. But people don't stop doing it, the same way they don't stop getting angry. It's an emotion."

"We're going tomorrow."

"But bus service is so much slower."

"Fuck it, we're going," she said. "And you can't blackmail me either."

"Why not?"

"Because you'll have to live with yourself as an emotionally fucked up human being. Can you live with that?"

"I got this far. Actually most people have gone this far. And further."

"It won't kill you."

The sick little kid from the television was to hold a press conference for his recent wish fulfillment: a once in a lifetime chance to receive some sort of sexual gratification from the celebrity of his choice. The charity foundation he signed up with had really expanded its reach.

Lillie wanted to attend the pointless briefing to see if she could get a word with the kid, get his blessing or something. So we went.

Kenny, the sick kid, was being treated in a mega-hospital, a multi-building complex that served as a combination hospital, rehab facility, cancer research lab, blood donation centre, Wal-Mart, and movie theatre.

The press briefing was being held in Kenny's hospital room. The fresh-faced freckled little freak sat atop his throne, his bus-sized hospital bed, where various wires, gadgets, IV poles, and milk machines surrounded him. He was the six million dollar man, but handicapped. We all jammed into his room. A handful of television reporters were in there with us. They all looked to be from other countries, states, provinces—cherry-faced nobodies reporting on a story for people who could share sympathy for Kenny from their living room sofas without giving up a dime for the hospital or charity foundation paying for his bed and complimentary teddy bear. Despite different languages, accents, and approaches, every report sounded the same.

Lillie was smiling and looked as if she was praying with her eyes open while everyone waited for Kenny to speak. Throughout the entire hubbub, no one had remembered to mention what he was dying from. The disease wasn't important, I supposed. The fact that this fresh-faced freckled little freak was soon to keel over and push up daisies was all that mattered. Kenny didn't look sick. He looked like a brat, actually. He had short crisp black hair and a natural puffy frown. He looked like those kids in school who told me to shut up a lot.

"Shut up, everyone," Kenny spoke.

People hushed as if a goat had been slaughtered.

"Let's get this shit over with," Kenny continued, his voice high strung, the words coming out in a child-like screech. "I have a wish to receive."

The room awed, swayed with a cutesy breath like we were floating on water. We were on the Titanic, and I was the only one who knew how it was going end.

A doctor stepped in; unnoticed, she stood beside me with a clipboard.

"Who's first?" Kenny asked.

"Hi there, Kenny! Sarah from FTBS, local CH affiliate, your number one action news team from the mid North Western area," said the reporter. Sarah had the mouth of a shark. Every time she talked, I expected shrimp to jam her throat.

Sarah dug into her purse and pulled out a pink teddy bear for Kenny. "This is for you," she said, "as a token of appreciation for your bravery."

"What bravery?" the doctor whispered.

"Great, I don't have one of those," Kenny said, throwing the thing into his pile of teddy bears.

"How does it feel, Kenny," Sarah continued, "to sit here about to have your wish fulfilled when doctors said you would never walk again?"

"I didn't say he couldn't, I said he shouldn't," the doctor said, barely audible. "I'm a doctor, for Christ's sake. I know what I'm talking about. But no, it's so much more miraculous to fit in some misinformation to sweeten this story even more. Just you watch, Kenny could walk fine for the next couple of years, then one day—boom—his kneecaps erode."

"Well," Kenny said with a smirk, "you don't need to walk to get a wish."

Everyone sighed deeply. One more breath and we'd all be vacuumed sealed in the hospital room.

The doctor banged her head against the clipboard.

The pre-planned, pre-determined feeding frenzy continued for fifteen arduous minutes, each reporter basically asking the same question. When it was over, Lillie and the other spiritual people in the room took the opportunity to get their blessings or whatever they had in mind. Maybe a lock of his hair?

I had had enough of Kenny.

I decided to explore the hospital grounds. I love hospitals. They remind me of downtowns, bus stations, airports, churches, concert events—they exude this sense that they're the centre of the universe. No one stopped me as I coasted through corridor after corridor. It sort of reminded me of high school, with the sense that this could be the end of my life. The only difference was the hospital staff, all of whom seemed far less worried than the students I once mingled with. I did wonder, however, what a place with such an entrenched sense of depression would be like if the staff had taken a little bit more time and money to spruce it up. In the Moscow Metro, artwork is hung in the subway cars. Perhaps the nursing staff could head over to IKEA, get some funky lamps, some pointless foldable furniture, some highly reproduced photographs of Paris or New York, maybe some plastic potted plants, coloured light bulbs, and children's sheets and spruce up the place. A patient could be given the sad news of a disease while sitting on an IKEA sofa that self-reflexively references its function as a thing to be sat on.

An old man shouted for me to stop as I passed his room.

"Are you a nurse?" he asked me as I stood in the doorway.

"Do I look like a nurse?"

"You look like an egotistical nobody. So you must be a nurse."

I kept walking. I found my way back to Kenny's room. Jesus of Wal-Mart, Aisle 3 was still conducting "the blessing." All the reporters were gone but the stereotypes had stayed behind. A woman in beads and flower patterned jeans looked like she was trying to steal the air Kenny was breathing. A bleached blonde handsome man appeared to be trying to fulfill a lack of spirituality in his life. There were some other people, too. Lillie was there, still smiling, no soul left in her eyes.

I managed to drag her away, all the way to the bus. The displeased doctor with the clipboard had come back anyway and was monopolizing Kenny.

We made it all the way to the bus before Lillie's smile dissolved into a disgusted frown. "What a fucking brat," she said, sitting down. "That Kenny kid. I can't believe that kid!"

"What'd he say?"

"It's not what he said. Through the entire briefing and small talk afterwards he was just majorly ego-tripping," she said. "A sick, dying boy! It makes me so frustrated."

"It's understandable."

"It shouldn't be."

"What's the problem?"

"Is someone going to tell that brat he's no big shot?"

"Uh . . . well . . . " I gulped.

"His parents maybe," she said. "I mean, come on. I saw them there too. Now those are some fucked up individuals. When I have a child, I'm going to make sure he's not going to grow up to be some stupid narcissist. He's worse than that celebrity person . . . the one who's fulfilling his stupid wish. What the fuck is up with that anyway? How does he know about that shit at fourteen?"

"Seems pretty common to me," I said.

"But this is different," Lillie said. "He's probably going to be like that forever, if he lasts that long."

"Honestly, I don't know what you're fretting about. He's exactly as I'd expect him to be," I said.

"What? Undeserving? A pretentious weakling? A fraud?"

"Now, now. He does actually have a disease."

"I know. But what if he didn't, though?"

"Then . . . he wouldn't?"

"No," she said, slapping me on the shoulder. "I mean, like, if he was lying."

"I don't think it's his decision to be diseased."

"I know! But imagine if it's just one big fraud, though. What are they gonna do? Arrest him?"

"You just don't like him," I said. "You're angry. You've also been watching way too much television."

"I'm angry because I've been watching too much television. How can you just accept that kid's behaviour?" Lillie continued.

"Those newscasts spouting unicorns and rainbows only ever cover cheery surfaces. I told you when we were watching it that it was nonsense."

"I'm sure not every sick kid is like Kenny," Lillie said.

"I know, but it's better to think they are, that everyone in the end is like Kenny."

Lillie turned to me, looked at me fully, as if for the first time. "That's fucking depressing."

"Will you shush, we're on a bus for fuck's sake," I pleaded.

"I don't give a shit, that's depressing," she said. "You actually want things to be that way?"

"What? No. I don't want that. Of course not. It's just the truth."

"I know that, but expecting people to be nice and empathetic is so much happier and better and of greater character."

"Yeah, but you see, when I come across someone nice, it's a pleasant surprise. But if they're bullshitters, I don't get hurt," I said.

"When you met me in the elevator, did you expect me to be a slut? A whore? An easy pick-up," Lillie asked.

I didn't want to talk. I wanted to glue my mouth. A man standing beside us asked an empty chair to spare some change.

"Well, you see, honey—"

"You've never called me honey," Lillie said.

"I honestly can't remember what I was thinking at the time," I replied.

"Fuck you," she said.

"Honest."

"I said fuck you."

"I opened myself up, did I not? Emotionally. And ultimately sexually as well, but you can't use that against me."

"That's your problem. You think being human is a weakness no matter what."

"What? No! I'm not an alien."

"You don't have to be. You don't expect much of yourself either," she said. "You would be in university right now if you did."

"I'll get a degree in defrauding the public eventually. Don't you like having me around?" I asked.

"I'd like to be around someone who doesn't look at me as an inflatable sex doll."

"I don't do that," I said. "Sex dolls aren't reusable, I don't think."

She glared at me.

"That's a bad joke. Sorry, just forget it."

"You're fucked," she said. "You know what my first thought was when I saw you? That you were the same sort of guy who sees me as some irresolvable mystery unless I help get his dick wet. The same sort of guy who thinks he's hot shit for noticing my eye colour. Was my first thought correct?"

My eyes rolled. I leaned back, wanting to fall asleep. We rode alone, in silence, amongst engine wheezes and sleazy drivers, breezy babes, broken roads, potholes, and a man asking an empty chair for spare change.

The next day after the hospital visit, Lillie stomped into my apartment (housed in Whitey McConcrete) and flopped down on our sofa, muscle detailing itself down the length of her arm as she turned on the television with a vehemence that nearly destroyed the remote. Kenny was fully forgotten.

"I hate capitalism," she blurted out.

I sat in front of her on our wooden coffee table, a piece of furniture thieved from Lillie's mother. "What did it do this time?" I asked.

"Xavier. Change your tone. I'm not a crying child missing my lollipop."

"What? I wasn't talking down to you. Talk to me. What happened?"

"Me and my friends," she continued, "we just got kicked out of a coffee shop for loitering. Now how the hell do you judge what constitutes loitering at a coffee shop. They also kicked out this kid who was like, writing or doing homework," Lillie said. "What if he's going to be the next Ernest Hemingway or Pierre Berton or whoever? They just kicked a creative person out of a place where people go to think and chat and do stuff like that."

"A coffee shop?" I said. "What does this have to do with capitalism?"

"That wouldn't have happened if independent shops could thrive," she said. "But no, everything in North America has to be a chain or a brand or a logo or a symbol. Everyone must be a customer because real people have souls, but consumers don't."

I stared at her.

"I don't want to get rid of capitalism," she continued.

"Then why did you just say you hated it a second ago?"

"I'm just going through that youthful anti-Western rebellion phase," she said. "Just warning you now, I might become an activist, but it'll be temporary."

"I understand. Nothing wrong with activism," I assured her, sitting beside her.

"But that is fucked up, getting kicked out for loitering," Lillie continued. "I mean, there's so many things wrong with that."

"I know, I know."

"Let's get our own place."

"Huh?" I stuttered. "Wait, why not go back to complaining about capitalism instead? That's much easier."

"Prove to me that capitalism can work by getting us a nice place where we can live together."

"What? Are you kidding? Did you just use that story to justify getting an apartment? Why would we want a new place?"

"Did you just seriously ask that? Look where we live. This place is a shit hole surrounded by concrete," Lillie said.

"You think I don't know that?" I said. "But it's home, and we've only been together for like four months."

"Six."

"I'll settle for five."

"It's six, Xavier," she said. "It's about time we prepare for our coming one year anniversary by finding a place. It might just take the next six months."

"Have you ever been in a relationship before?" I asked.

"Have you?"

"I had a one night stand once."

"Whatever," she said. "What's the problem with thinking ahead?" I rolled my eyes and went to the kitchen to make a sandwich. "Did you hear me?" Lillie asked.

"Oh, look, capitalism has caused us to buy sub-standard mayonnaise," I said. "And filthy Mexican lettuce grown next to an asbestos factory in Texas. How about this, I'll prove capitalism works by buying food that isn't shit."

"Xavier," she shouted, "don't ignore me here. We can afford a better place. Your job at the . . . at the . . ."

"Oh, don't worry about not remembering. I wish I could forget about it too, every morning when I wake up," I said. "I work in the horse stable at Medieval Times."

"Right, well, animals are nice."

"Where did you get that idea? Did you add *Animal Planet* to our satellite package?"

"If we got a new place, we would still have money left over to get married."

I stopped and stepped back out into the living room empty-handed. I laughed, artificially. "Mark your fucking calendar; we're not getting married."

"Guys say that all the time. We will eventually. I can feel it," she said.

"Well, I can't. We're not, let me repeat, we're not getting—"

"Why not?" Lillie interrupted me.

"Because it's pointless. It's a waste of money. It's conformist. It's retarded. It's fake. It's plastic, bad food, worse music, stupid cheers, stupid laughter."

"It's love."

"It's capitalism, Lillie. Right?"

"No, it isn't, it's tradition."

"Fuck tradition," I said. I headed back to the kitchen to scavenge for other foods. Lillie followed.

"You're just in a mood because of your parents," she said. "Just because your mom and dad couldn't figure out their marriage or whatever they called it, doesn't mean we can't have a successful one."

"Oh, yes, it does. You're too young anyway."

"What is that supposed to mean?" she asked.

"I don't know, but I hear it all the time. Thought I'd try to apply it to something," I said. "Now that I think about it, it is a stupid phrase."

"Xavier, focus, please." She walked up to me and clutched my hands.

"It's all bullshit though," I continued. "At the pace society goes these days, age grants shit all."

"Xavier!" she said. "I'm asking you to take me seriously as a human being, as the one human being you'll always love."

I stared at her. I looked around the shabby apartment she wanted me to reject and then down at the ring finger she was seeking for me to tag with a simple circle of mineral.

"I'm going to start looking for places," she said. "You start figuring out how to pay for it."

"You know what's sexy these days? Women who have financial control."

"Oh, yeah, I mean the phrase makes me horny just hearing it," Lillie joked. "You make more money right now, so you have greater security."

"But this is my apartment."

"That your parents have helped to pay for. You must figure it out this time."

"I regret it already. Except for the 'you' part, of course," I said.

"Just stop thinking of your parents, please," she said, walking away.

"Didn't we start out talking about capitalism?" I shouted. "You're the one that brought it up."

"I'm going back out with friends. See you later," Lillie said.

The front door shut. An echoing silence.

"Bye," I whispered.

Monday was the next morning, and it was the only day, as I recall, that Lillie and I didn't have to work. While many others awoke to awkward yawning—day-old coffee and donuts, shower spray made up of a mysterious substance they tried to pass off as "water"—we got to devote our Monday morning hours to enjoying the little things in life, like ignoring each other.

On that particular Monday, however, I'd been awakened early by Lillie's exaggerated energy for home hunting, which I, of course, was quick to remind her was complete optimistic claptrap. We would be lucky enough if we found a *liveable* (and I used that term broadly) living space over the next couple of months, let alone in the next couple of minutes. Regardless, it seemed the day itself didn't want to be good to me either. I slumped onto the stolen sofa, fresh from a shower of "water," and stretched out the Monday paper. It seemed that language was beginning to get on people's nerves. Maybe there would be a revolt. While patrons in Quebec City protested the use of English language signage in French restaurants, Vancouverites were complaining about prostitutes being treated like human beings. The front page, however, was devoted to some sexual affair of some federal politician who was now being badgered by the politically ill-informed citizenry who were disturbed that a public official's private life was not fulfilling his ridiculous image—that politicians should be icons of virtue.

My coffee went cold from neglect.

Lillie and I hit the town, with me mostly following. Given that I had been raised in a place where direction was irrelevant, I had a mental picture of a map of Toronto I had lost and subsequently forgotten about. Lillie and I were on the subway heading towards the Annex, or Bloor West Village, or Mirvish Village or perhaps even Mississauga for all I knew.

Wherever we were going, Lillie had something on her mind. "Did you tell your parents we were home-hunting?" she asked.

"No."

"Good."

"Good?"

"People tend to relive the lives of their parents."

"For God's sake," I rubbed my eyes. "Lillie, I don't live in an indie film where my life centres around a cutesy form of dysfunctionality. If that's even a word. You get what I'm saying?"

"I know that. I was just making sure."

"I don't like talking to my parents, so why would I tell them I'm about to turn down more places to live?" I asked.

"We're going to find a place."

"To reject."

"To live in," Lillie persisted. "And how could you hate your parents? That's awful. I'm sure they sacrificed a lot."

"Their sex life."

"Their what life?"

"Wait, I didn't say I hated them. I said I don't like talking to them. Monumental difference," I said.

"Right, of course. Get up, this is our stop," Lillie said.

We stepped out towards white tile. Sheep herding filled my mind. "You know what, why don't we talk about your parents for a change," I said, "because you know what I hate more than my parents apparently?"

"What, Xavier?" she rolled her eyes.

"Talking about my parents. There are other fucked up people my life revolves around too."

"Like me."

"Like you," I said. "How is Sarnia doing these days? Still pissed off for being named after the kissing capital of the world?"

"My mother's name is Fiona," she said. "Have you ever met them?" Lillie asked.

We stepped out into weather, air, a thing called oxygen. "No," I answered.

"Then it'll be a nice surprise when they come over to our new place," Lillie smiled, her heart seemingly filled with sugary cereal.

Lillie's optimism was far from a manufactured gift card. It was understandable. She had known only the inside of Whitey McConcrete. It was her childhood home—apartment, balcony, whatever—her entire life spent inside its confines.

We came across our first open house on a furiously quiet one-way street, parked hybrid cars linked bumper to bumper on one side. We shook hands with the real estate agent.

"Hello," the agent shrieked. "And you are Mr. and Mrs. . . ?"

"Flubber," I answered.

"Really?" the agent looked perplexed. "Is that Finnish?"

"Sure," I said. "You see in my language, Finnish, there is no 'r' sound, like rubber. It just doesn't exist. So if I translate my original last name, my Finnish accented parents would pronounce it 'Wubber'."

"Really?"

"Oh, yes," I continued. "Can't have that, though, so I took it upon myself for the sake of my family when I mastered English, taught by none other than the nephew of the man who invented the dictionary, to change it to something easier, more dignified."

"More dignified?" she smiled.

"Tell her," Lillie blurted out, "about the time you learned geometry from the great-great-great second cousin of the man who invented the triangle."

I blinked, flinched, smiled. "Why don't we get to a tour?" the agent said, or more or less demanded. "You seem like a young couple eager to start a new and modern life."

"In that case, we should move on then," I said, "because if I'm not mistaken, this house was constructed before the founding of sliced bread."

"Go," Lillie pushed me.

"That would be Victorian architecture," the agent informed us as we headed into the living room. "We're in a neighbourhood filled with wonderful heritage, cemented by the largest number of Victorian-era homes in North America."

"So it's conformist?" I said.

"Shut up," Lillie hissed.

"You know, dear, that's actually a very rude thing to say, and I wish people would say it less often," I said.

"I love the atmosphere in here," Lillie smiled at the agent, moving past me. "It's so open, there's air, and yet it's cozy, too."

"Yes, it has three bedrooms, an open concept kitchen; it's a duplex, with a very nice business couple as neighbours," the agent said. "Four bathrooms."

"Four?" I said. "But there's only two floors."

"Yes."

"The fourth's like, for a dog or something?"

"There's a backyard."

"So . . . no?"

"He's adverse," Lillie said.

"To spending money," I added. "How much is this place?"

"Prices will be negotiated by seriously interested buyers only," the agent said.

"What if only half of two customers actually show serious interest?"

We were asked to leave for wasting valuable time. We walked a bit to find another open house down the same one-way street, the same hybrid cars parked parallel. I managed to eye a gas-guzzling four-door street-legal monster truck crammed into a self-made garage. Lillie stopped, kissed me, told me she loved me.

"I love you too," I assured her, "but that place back there was clearly pushing seven digits."

"I know that; I didn't expect to buy it. I don't expect to buy anything, actually."

"What?" I was shocked.

"I'm only doing this because I never have," Lillie said, her voice soft and eyes glassy. "This is just us two, let's make it fun."

I was expressionless. "Are you playing on my sympathies?"

"Are you using me for sex?"

We found a five-storey condominium building with round balconies, screaming for youthful post-modern couples to cover its façade in flags, posters, potted plants, fantastic rainbow paint. I faked having no interest this time around. Our new agent, however, did not have to fake his own interest. He could care less, told us to do our own goddamned tour.

The place was off to a good start with us. Only one bathroom, and furnished accordingly with one of those old fashioned novelty tubs you'd have found on the Titanic. Judging by its condition, it looked as if it had been raised from the bottom of the sea. It was comforting to see that someone had had the smarts to put home fashion sense one slight step above hygiene. There was one thing nagging me, though.

I decided to scout out the balcony, the oddly perfectly spherical balcony. Lillie joined me several minutes later.

"Look at that," I said, opening my arms towards the sky. "Look at this view." It was spectacular. "We're only five floors up, yet it's like we're on the edge of space."

"It's certainly a plus," she admitted. "But that view isn't the apartment."

"Exactly."

"Exactly what?"

"This is important. I mean at night," I said, misty eyed. I put my arms around her waist; she eyed me suspiciously. "It's the most romantic place in this city."

She smiled.

"We could do it on the balcony and no one would notice," I whispered.

"Well hopefully," she said, "but I think we should focus more on the place we'll be spending most of our time in."

"You buy the apartment, I'll rent out the balcony."

"I mean, this place is within range." Lillie broke free, and stood in the doorway. "Sure it's more expensive for less space, but it's closer to your work and other better jobs."

"Yeah, but one thing ruins it all."

"That's not possible."

"It's boring."

"It's boring?"

"You don't think so?" I said. "Look at it. Either everything is in its rightful place, or someone placed it in the wrong place on purpose."

"You have got to be kidding."

"It's a valid complaint."

"What's so exciting about where we live now?"

"Everything," I replied. "Every week the fire alarm gets pulled for no reason. The garage door regularly won't open. The front lawn has tire tracks from drunk driving exercises. Squirrels are fished out of the basement pool. A man was fished out of the front fountain. That chandelier once fell down, too."

"Xavier, that's not exciting."

"Well, what do you call it?"

"I don't know," Lillie answered. "Life."

"Life is pretty boring."

"No, it isn't," she said. "It's damn exciting. I am not content living in that apartment if it only serves to give you or anyone else interesting things to write about in your diary every night."

I tried to smile but failed. The wind was picking up.

"I see what you're doing here," Lillie continued. "You think I'm just the regular levelheaded girl fighting back against the bad boy antics of a street kid."

"I'm from the suburbs, actually."

"I know," she said. "It's all just a plot to you. I don't have to be some ridiculous stereotype to be serious about my life or about where I want to live, whether it's boring or not. I know that sometimes it seems people around us want to live in a movie, where every guy is a deep sea diver who's also emotional, and every girl is a stripper by night and a bikini model by day, but I'm not a character, and neither are you."

The lighthearted tone in my heart sparked its last flicker as my soul, or something that felt like a soul, sputtered smoke. I decided against admitting to her that before she came along, one night stands were the sparse but only order for my sexual passion.

"Will you marry me?" I asked her.

Lillie laughed. She walked back into the gloom.

Lillie went back home but I decided to walk. I walked downtown under the shade of stores and high rises.

I watched suits and skirts stream out of office towers towards trams and trains, cafeteria lines and beer bottles, bar stools, and bottomless TV programming—and I realized I could either join them or sit and continue watching, powerless. What was so inconceivable was trying to imagine what it would be like if all people could just start over, remove the basement we'd been building on top of for so long, remove all the traditions, the entrenched schizophrenia and superstition, the wives' tales and weary logic, the pollution and overpopulation, the embarrassing cultural clichés and generational norms. Maybe then we all wouldn't be so weak.

I felt right but not well. I had unknowingly been walking in circles for over an hour. I needed to go home. I needed to stop thinking.

Waiting for a streetcar in Chinatown, I stood in linear fashion with a few other frustrated nobodies. Lights were ablaze atop a fire truck parked in front of an eatery across the street. Three firemen rushed in. Not an uncommon sight for a place that prides itself on selling animal fat as food.

A middleaged woman to my right appeared to be talking to an imaginary friend beside her. "Finally!" she said, meaning the arrival of an ambulance alongside the fire truck. "I had to call them, emergency," she continued, pointing to no one. Two paramedics carrying various supplies walked into the restaurant. The woman, who had written in white-out "Little" on her ball cap next to the word "Ninja", bragged aloud about the person she had apparently saved.

"You don't do that. You don't drink a full bottle of Listerine," she said. "You don't. He stepped out, and plunk, dropped straight to the floor."

A streetcar came that wasn't the one I was looking for. The woman got on. It pulled away. I watched the three firemen and two paramedics come out again emptyhanded, laughing with a discomforting frustration.

No one was sick. No one was there. Should I have told the woman about her imaginations? Where would someone get Listerine at an eatery anyway?

To my left at the streetcar stop was a recently-introduced-to-puberty young couple. The boy was bathed in checker-patterned clothing, shorts and a short sleeved t-shirt. His collar was propped up, engulfing most of his neck. Massive mirrored sunglasses shrouded his eyes and most of his face. His hair was drowning in gel and spiked upwards against the direction of gravity. He looked like a cartoon character who didn't realize he was a cartoon. The girl was painted in makeup and piercings. Her attempt to look twenty-one? Some bad grammar and a high-pitched voice might betray whatever age she was pretending to be. She was wearing barely anything, a rather revealing white tank top and jean shorts purposely curled up to show as much of the thigh as possible before public indecency laws would kick in.

They talked about what they'd eaten, commercials or ads they'd seen, people they liked to stereotype or belittle, how perfect they themselves were as human specimens, and how much money they had borrowed from their well-off parents. I was being siphoned into a place of hate, of ageism, of hating people who are easy to hate.

I waited until an empty streetcar came along. I hopped on one painted to look like an oversized beer bottle, and began reading advertisements to get my daily dose of philosophical insight. "The sun always rises in the East," read one. "Why not block it with a deck attachment retractable parasol!" "Are you tired of living . . ." I saw, did a double take, " . . . paycheck to paycheck?" I started to think back to that little fact I remembered reading about, that jumpers on the Golden Gate bridge usually point East. The sun always rises in the East, and people look to the light for enlightenment, for understanding, for hope. Are the jumpers hopeful?

I rang the ringer, walked a bit, found a bridge. It overlooked a river, two highways, and some railroad tracks.

But I didn't jump. I went back to watch the suits and skirts pass by a coffee shop window, to feel happy I still had the freedom and breath to notice them as faces, albeit faceless faces.

Lillie broke up with me several months later. Off she went to an unknown location, leaving me with Whitey McConcrete as my only companion.

Over an unmentionable length of time, the true far-sightedness it took to live in Whitey McConcrete came to light. I grew to hate the place, its face, the smirk it made as I dove below its immovable concrete awning. Its cracks, the fatigue it suffered, became blatantly apparent. After Lillie left, it was high time I built up the metaphorical balls it would take to move out on my own, again. It was time to find a more suitable architectural disaster to live in, a new face for my nightmares.

Grudgingly, I asked Mother for help. We were at her condo computer desk. "Now I'm finally going to be able to say goodbye to my son," she said, "as he moves on to the next stage of his life."

"Wonderful."

"You'll love it. My parents did the same thing for me, but you're lucky. They hosted a big party for me with all my friends."

"Even though by then you clearly didn't believe in God and they did?"

"They didn't care about that."

"You know Dad doesn't give a shit about me moving," I said.

"Your father's too busy at the moment babysitting that little windbag."

"His second wife."

"She goes by that as well," Mother said. "He should be here with us. I even invited him."

"Nicely?"

"Of course nicely. He said no, said he's getting her car fixed."

"I guess those things need to be done."

"Xavier, don't think for a minute that you're not allowed to get angry at him for missing out on this opportunity," she said, swivelling around in her swivel chair.

"I think you can do that for the both of us," I said.

"We worked so hard together to be a family when you were younger," she continued, "and then he goes and acts as if his job were done."

"I appreciate your guys' work. I mean, even at night, you weren't finished. You continued that hard work, only this time in bed."

"Yes, yes, we know. It wasn't our fault the walls were paper thin," she said, "but, seriously, you can get angry."

"Later. Have you found anything?" I asked.

Mother clicked off the webpage. "You were an angry kid in high school."

"I think the correct term is young adult."

"And you never let it all go, or at least we never saw you let it go," she said. Her computer rattled, plunked, wheezed like a robot with gas. "It doesn't matter what you did, what matters is—"

"That I find a home, of course, I'm totally with you there," I interrupted. "I think your computer went into hibernation."

Mother slowly swivelled back to her keyboard and the real estate listings. She proceeded to suggest many an overpriced monstrosity, hard to maintain brick shithouses that were taller than two telephone poles. I, as the foolish home buyer, brought up cheap apartment buildings, most reduced in price because of ongoing police investigations.

"How about this one?" Mother asked.

"Too pretentious," I said.

"Who cares?"

"I do."

"What's wrong with being pretentious?" she asked.

"What's wrong with driving a Hummer?" I replied.

"You've got a better job than you used to, better security, better money. It's within range, it's a nice neighbourhood. Admittedly, it does seem the previous owners cared about looks over living, but you can change that with a little elbow grease."

"What about that place?" I said, clicking. "Look at that."

"It's above a computer liquidator."

"Exactly. It has no exterior."

"You could buy a new mattress with how much it costs."

"So it's cheap."

"Too cheap." Mother pulled up its history and read, "Formerly the home of a book burning fraternity, the place has been vacant since 1983 when the group renting it was arrested on domestic terrorism charges."

"A book burning fraternity?"

"One bathroom, one bedroom, oversized living room/kitchen," she read on, "5% discount on the store below. Must be tolerant of loud noises because once a week the building welcomes a men's book club."

"Salt in the wounds."

"This is an awful place," Mother said.

"Sounds exciting," I replied.

"By what measure?"

"Well, what else is there?"

Mother clicked around. The printer came to life, puked out a page. She handed it to me. "Here," she said, "here's exciting. Let's go check it out."

We jolted forth in search of this slice of excitement. Constructed from old thrown out wooden box cars from the early 1900s, this home was three floors high and at one time had been a shelter for immigrants unable to speak a word of English. Its massive rooms yet tiny bathrooms, kitchen, and living room were ideal for the quick stop traveller. The place still had the plaque bearing its inscribed nickname on the wall: Immigrant Haus. The street the house was once right next to had been torn up in the 1950s. Back then, people were under the impression that prosperity was infectious. Immigrant Haus was thus shut down— walled up by overly optimistic ideologies held by those who were dissatisfied with spreading an under-realized image of perfection. A new major downtown thoroughfare went right past Immigrant Haus, but due to an increasing space crunch, the area that would have been its lawn was filled with brick corner stores and shops. A small four-storey office block in the 70s was directly connected to Immigrant Haus's east wall. The whole structure was reopened as cheap temporary housing some years later.

There it was surrounded on all sides by stores of various diversities, from every angle its third floor the only thing that could be seen, and only reachable by a small alleyway in between brick walls. A black steel staircase leading up to the third floor was the only way in. Its old front door was walled up to make a niche for a much needed dumpster. Yet even with such surroundings, and it now sporting only an inauspicious two windows, the old artistic trim from the 1900s still decorated the only floor that could be seen from the outside, giving it a kind of localized grandeur.

Mother and I stood across the street, peering up at that third floor. We were awestruck. "That is so cool," I said.

"Why didn't they ever tear it down?" Mother asked.

"Says here that after the house was boarded up, a now defunct historical society successfully saved Immigrant Haus from destruction," I read. "Apparently the place stands as a testament to the immigrants who still work tirelessly in this city."

"And now you want to live in it."

"And now I want to live in it."

"You don't think a hometown boy moving in is a bit of an insult?"

"Maybe if the minutemen moved in, yes."

"Why do you want it?"

"I like the location," I answered. "This place is genuine. That's real wood, that's a real image. Even after so many years, it's still standing, maybe not strongly, but still."

"But you can't see most of it. How will you get mail?" Mother asked.

"I'll figure it out," I said. "I've already fallen in love."

"It is historic."

"Yes, the first building in Toronto to be logically in the middle of nowhere."

"Why don't we check inside first?"

"It says here the now defunct historical society did nothing to Immigrant Haus inside or out in the years they had it under their ownership," I read on.

"That's bad."

"That's a plus."

"What?"

"No one tampered with it," I said.

"I'd be surprised if it had electricity," Mother said.

We walked over, through the ill lit alleyway, and up the steel staircase to the third floor door. It was unlocked. The place was yellow inside, very yellow, with black writing on specific spots on the walls. Dates, names, quick accounts—the long sent text messages of another time. On one piece of the floor beam I noticed a locomotive logo from one of the box cars that had given its life over to be built into this house. The place was dusty, rundown, ruined, and in the longterm undoubtedly unliveable.

"This is fantastic!" I said.

"It is quite exciting," Mother replied, walking in circles. "But you can't live on excitement."

"Sure I can," I said. "Young people today."

"This place is awful," she said, "and if I know you, you're not going to do anything to improve it."

"That would ruin it."

"It's already ruined."

"Yes, isn't it wonderful?"

"What if it collapses? This place is dangerous."

"Oh, only slightly," I said. "The floorboards look to be giving into gravity too easily. So do the walls. But there's nowhere else like this. I could say I don't live on the grid."

"No one is going to want to live with you," Mother said.

"That's the way I like it."

"You know, I had always wondered why Lillie broke up with you," she said, "but now it's pretty obvious."

"I wouldn't bring anyone back to this place anyway."

"Why?"

"They'd only wreck it," I said. "This place was a home for people's greatest moments of loneliness, of feeling forgotten. It'd be an insult to infringe on that tradition."

"You're a stickler for tradition?"

"Only those I want to respect."

"I don't like this."

"I'm buying it," I said.

"Why?"

"Hey, at least if this fails, it will be my own fault; my failures will be my own."

"Oh? And what were they before?"

"An imprint."

A couple of days later I was fully wedged into my new home. Instead of stealing my parents' furniture again, I stole some lumber and built everything from scratch. The hydro, water, and structural integrity were, of course, sub-par beyond imagination, but in checking the records, amazingly, I saw that the last time repairs were needed, the boxcars were still being dismantled for the home's floorboards. Due to the pollution and fumes from the adjacent one-star steakhouse, pharmacy, and office building, termites and other parasites became non-existent. I knew I had found the home for the rest of my life—the home that would be my ascent to adulthood, or something like that. If I was going to be honest, it seemed I might have simply been thinking goofily because of the grease cloud the wind ushered in from the fast food restaurants. But that ascent to adulthood thing gave me some dignity so I went with that instead.

★

I am sound asleep in the passenger seat, flying high in my dreams from sniffing the seat leather for too long. I am about to lay waste to my childhood enemies, having completed my ultimate fantasy of transforming into a bomb-breathing dragon, when Felix taps me on the shoulder.

"Wake up," he says.

I shuffle in my seat and mumble something about the fantastical world of destruction I wish to remain in.

"Were you dreaming?" Felix asks.

"Reconnecting with God," I say. "What's the problem?"

"This book of yours is rubbish. It has more holes than Tupac."

"I don't know what you're talking about."

"You wrote this in the past tense, right?" he says. "But you wrote it as if everything is coming at you at that particular moment."

"And what's wrong with that?"

"I don't know what the fuck is going on. You don't know the name of someone one minute, yet the next you do. Just go back and change it. You won't have to just say shit all of a sudden that contradicts what's happening."

"That's just how I roll."

"Whatever happened to Lillie? You know it's customary in autobiographies to say what happened to the people in your life, linearly. She didn't just fall off the face of the earth."

"I don't really care about her, that was a long time ago."

"But she plays a major role."

"I'll make a note of it," I say.

"You are an angry individual," Felix says. "On Tyler Durden's scale of anger with 1/10 being a willingness to punch oneself in the kidney and 10/10 being an inviolable need to blow up a building, you appear to be around 5. Maybe even a 5 1/2. Have I ever told you that?"

"Have I ever told you that you're an idiot?"

"Exactly my point," he says.

"What does 5/10 even mean? Trip a toddler?"

"I'd say snuff out people you don't like."

I laugh. "People terrify me," I say, "but not enough for me to harm anyone."

Felix shakes his head.

"She had no reason to leave me," I say. "I can legitimately get angry over that."

"Xavier," Felix says, matter-of-factly, "Lillie wanted to be with her family. I thought that would be obvious."

"Who the hell would want their family?"

"You might have had bad parents, but a lot of other people managed to get stuck with family they truly like to be with."

"I can't imagine."

"No, obviously you can't."

"Thanks for the book update. Can you get back to it?"

"Sounds like reconciliation is a tall but needed order for you, my friend."

A glare is growing in the laminated glass, glossy from the polyvinyl butyral concoction that keeps car windshields intact in case of spider-web fractures. The glare travels across the front windshield at alien spaceship speeds and will soon orbit far beyond our plane if the halo is not stopped or hailed down. I can see Felix's excitement at the possibility of other contact. His thumb was a bookmark in my manuscript but now it grips the steel wheel. The white pages wash over one another. The Red Sea no longer resists Moses' passing. Felix furiously roles down his windshield.

"Get out of the car and flag him down," he says.

"I don't want to," I say. "It's too dangerous on the highway, like you said."

"This is the first fuckin' car we've seen all night."

"The tow truck will be here eventually," I say, "and besides, you haven't finished reading. Plus we don't even know if this guy can help us."

"Anyone is good."

"Even a serial killer? You know out here there's probably more murderous humans per capita then murderous animals."

"Don't be a pussy and just wave him down," he says.

"Let's leave this guy alone, we don't need to bother him."

"Nonsense, I bet he's an old farmer out for a drive on his usual route looking for people exactly like us."

"Pig feed."

"Tourists, newbies, people fresh out of luck," Felix says.

"Please. This is the forest, not Europe."

"He might be able to help us."

"Right, he'll have an extra tank of gas from his human fed wood chipper just for us," I say.

"Maybe he's a mechanic. Maybe he can tell us if there's something wrong with the car," Felix says.

"He's not going to say anything we don't already know."

"How about we just say hello and see how he's doing?" Felix says, turning to me. "Do you have a problem with us just having a little chat with a fellow human being? Beside, if he is a murderer, this is our chance to be heroes and catch a crook."

"You're living in a fantasy."

"Whatever, dragon boy."

"You made out my mumble?!"

Felix sticks his head out the window, only to be greeted by the same black canvas I encountered when we first stalled. There is nothing there. The car's red stop lights are shrinking disks in the rear windshield, perfect circles in the rearview mirror. That wonderful moist ripple sound of car tires rotating at several kilometres an hour can be heard dwindling as the car crests hill after hill behind us. Felix gently sits back in his seat, leaving the window open. The air seeps in and rescues us from the smell of aging wood trim and leather.

I try to get comfortable again. I re-prepare the dream landscape I had been wrongly awoken from but find images of bikini girls and Lillie in lingerie popping up above hilltops I could've sworn I'd already scorched with fiery breath. It's not a significant problem. Felix silently and slowly thumbs his way through the manuscript, looking for his place. He must have found where he had left of because he twirls the clipped pages back and continues reading.

CHAPTER ? (Find place for it later): CHILDHOOD

The first pet I owned was a goldfish in a spherical bowl when I was five years old. It swam in circles around flat, plastic, moulded-like-flowing seaweed that sprouted from multi-coloured aquarium sand. The bowl also had a little stone cave where my goldfish could have its fish dreams and contemplate fish suicide. My fish's bowl sat on a children's dresser drawer across from my bed. I would have to remind my father to feed my goldfish because I wasn't nearly tall enough to reach the top of the bowl. He also had to clean the bowl. I would watch as my father brought it to the washroom, trapped the fish in a plastic cup, rinsed out the old water, refilled the bowl with fresh tap water, and then poured my goldfish back in. We only got to clean the bowl a couple of times before the fish died because we either overfed it or forgot to clean the water. I can't remember what killed my goldfish.

The second pet I owned was a hamster my mother bought. It lived in a blue cage on a desk in a hallway. It lived a traditional, happy hamster life. It had a metal wheel to run on, a bed of wood chips to sleep in, a bowl of food to eat, a water bottle to drink from, and a plastic hamster ball I always wanted him to run in so that I could chase him around the house. He must have found this a torturous experience because he always tried to bite me. I never learned. A week after a bite I'd be back to sticking my fingers in his cage.

We had the hamster for about two years before he died of something. I remember my mother with the hamster wrapped in a towel on my parents bed, trying to understand why it was dying. It was obvious it was dying, but I kept forgetting. I'd run into my parents' room and jump up and down on the same bed my dying hamster was resting on, before my mother would shout for me to stop and leave, reminding me that the hamster was dying. I didn't own any pets for a long time after that.

Around the same time, a friend of mine lived on the 15th floor of an apartment building in the north end of the city. I loved going out on the balcony. I was both afraid and absorbed by the height. I would watch the cars, buses, and people down below squirm across the suburban landscape. I also enjoyed watching the pigeons nesting on the balcony ledge, looking for bread and other handouts. They'd eye the balcony gardens, the flower beds and tomato plants before being shooed away by adults that didn't enjoy their company. Flying rats.

I went out onto the balcony one day to find a pigeon's nest tucked in a far corner with two spotty grey eggs nestled in its centre. The mother was nowhere to be seen. I rushed back in to get my friend, and we went back out onto the balcony to inspect the eggs closer. They were fascinating little orbs of magic, like space rocks or million year old fossils, symbols of something so much larger than us squeezed to the size of a pebble. I gently grabbed one of the eggs with my tiny fingers. It felt hollow yet weighty. It had a peculiar warmth to it as if it were radioactive, as if the egg really had descended from outer space. The egg suddenly fell from my fingers and hit the balcony pavement. I had only been holding it about an inch above the ground, but it was a cliff's height to the delicate thing. It shattered across its equator, the yellow fetus of a pigeon spilling out headfirst across the balcony floor. I could make out its wings and undeveloped eyes. My friend and I ran back into the apartment, leaving my mess behind.

I'm in my public school playground on a Saturday with Nick and Bob scouring the field for lost marbles. Nick is a shapeshifter. He's on every grade school sports team. He has curly hair when it rains, straight when it's dry, blonde in the sun, brown in the winter. He is of average height. His middle name is John. We are in Grade 4 or 5 and on recess. Bob is the guy who will be friends with anyone.

Marbles are the poker chips of the schoolyard casino. In a fifteen minute break between classes, a dozen or so glossy orbs will change hands under the purview of unwritten laws. Two or more players agree to these rules just before play, like whether the game is for "funnies" or "keepsies." Every once in a while I'll have to scour the crisp, poorly fed grass just beyond the barely marked baseball diamond for marbles chucked or lost from past games. I look for handouts because I do not have the courage to ask my mother to buy me a bag of marbles, not that I believe she's able to afford it anyways. I do this sort of thing all the time. Trading cards, playing cards, pogs, marbles—it doesn't matter. I wait for other kids to give them away or to no longer find them fun and then swoop in and snatch them up. Schoolyard welfare trickling down to kids like me by anonymous parents willing to open up their wallets. When I can't get a handout, I scour the grass for those marbles that got away.

I have to search for marbles because of what happened the week before. Last Sunday when the neighbourhood was empty and the playground deserted I came across a kid my age with black curly mullet hair and a plain white t-shirt with the short sleeves curled up to his shoulders. We nicknamed these kids Welfare because they talked like yokels and dressed in tacky shirts from beer companies. Of course, this described most of the students at my school.

At the time, I had a handful of marbles and challenged Welfare to a game of keepsies. The point of marbles is to simply start far enough away from a small dimple in the hard sand and try to get both marbles, one from each player, into the dimple. The kid that gets both in successfully wins the pot. Welfare won the first game. And the second. And the third. I kept playing until I ran out of marbles. Welfare told me he'd give me back some of the marbles I'd lost if I did one thing. He climbed a tree just beyond the playground's fence. The tree had the old remnants of an incomplete tree house with flat wooden beams nailed between the tree's three largest branches. Welfare told me to climb up. I climbed up and perched myself on one end of a wooden beam that stretched out over an enormous gap to one of the tree's other large branches. Welfare told me he'd give me some of his marbles if I walked across the beam.

I told him I didn't want to do that. It was a flimsy, rotten piece of wood that had weathered countless Canadian seasons for God knows how long. He repeated his dare. I told him again that I really didn't want to do that, but the thought of free marbles kept me from simply giving up, climbing back down, and going home. I sat on the flimsy beam of wood, feeling its splinters, testing its strength. Welfare waited on the other side of the beam. Finally, I stretched my arms along as much of the beam as my little body would allow and swiftly dragged myself across, rubbing my ass over the old rotten wood. I breathed a sigh of relief when I reached the other side. Welfare jumped down from the tree. I asked him to give me some marbles. He laughed and said no and then ran home.

By the time I reach the uneven pavement of the school's basketball court with its netless hoops, I've found no marbles and neither have my friends. They could be lying. They could have pocketed their finds to avoid splitting the bounty. I'm sure Nick is preparing his slur cannon in case I question him or talk back. Suddenly, a weenie in an orange shirt pedals around the corner on his bicycle. He screeches to a stop on the other side of the basketball court and looks at the three of us. He has ash blonde hair that sprouts from the top of his head and flops over his eyes like spaghetti. I recognize him as a student from French Immersion, the students we never talk to or see. He cycles off down the court and around the building.

"He's such a loser," Nick says. "His face looks like an Aunt Mary."

"Do you know him?" Bob asks.

"He's Welfare's cousin," Nick says.

A couple of seconds after disappearing around the corner on his bike, Welfare's cousin rounds the corner again and zooms past the basketball court. He disappears around the school, and roughly the same amount of seconds later he again rounds the corner, zooms past the basketball court, and disappears behind the school.

"What is he doing?" Bob asks.

"What a bean flicker," Nick says.

Welfare's cousin rounds the corner again. As he passes in front of the basketball court for the fourth time, Nick picks up the basketball and hurls it at him. It strikes his bicycle's front tire and he tumbles to the ground. His helmet hits the ground with an eerie crack and his bicycle squeals as it bounces across the pavement. There's a slight delay between Welfare's cousin hitting the ground and his crying and moaning from seeing his bloody hands. His crying pierces the soundless suburb, like screeching train brakes. Bob makes a beeline and runs away. Nick goes and retrieves his basketball and then comes back to his spot beside me.

"Did you see that?" he says, smiling.

"Why did you do that?" I ask.

"I don't know."

"Does he have a dad?"

"Probably."

"Does his dad get angry?"

"I think so."

"How angry do you think he's going to be when Welfare's cousin tells him about what happened?" I say.

Nick and I gasp and run away, leaving Welfare's cousin to clean himself up.

In winter, I chucked snowballs at things. On weekends when we went to the grocery store, father would start the car and then go back inside the house to wait for it to warm up. I would stay outside and throw snowballs. Once, I was throwing snowballs at our little car imagining it was a fortress only I could defeat. I'd take cover in the mountainous snow and chuck snowballs I'd form from beneath my feet. I could hear the rustle of pebbles from the unfinished walkway that cleaved our front lawn into two equal halves. I picked up some snow, saw the gleaming stones, formed a rough sphere and launched the snowball at my imaginary enemy's central command, which happened to be the passenger seat window. It smacked the tempered glass with that satisfying thump, and then the window fractured. The entire pane, though, stayed in place. A million little shards of glass clung to one another, refusing to fall, refusing to shower glass upon the poorly shovelled driveway. That pinch of sound, that distressing crack of glass, looped in my mind. I didn't want to tell Father because I didn't want him to know that I had done something wrong.

I stared at the fractured window and its million little bits for a good five minutes until Mother and Father walked out. I didn't know what to do so I didn't do anything. I acted normal. I climbed into the back seat, my adolescent cranium only inches from a fractured car window, and slipped on my seatbelt. The click from the locking seatbelt seemed louder than I remembered. My head felt unusually hot underneath the thin layer of fabric of a bargain-bin black tuque. Father got into the driver's seat and Mother got in the passenger seat, and said nothing. They looked so normal.

We puttered out of our driveway and coughed down the potholed street of a suburban warzone: cars propped on cinder blocks, rusting construction equipment blocking sidewalks, snow-plough salt eating asphalt. I glanced out the corner of my eye at the fractured window. It jumped and bopped in its black rubber frame, creaked and squealed like train brakes screaming for release. I looked at my parents. They stared straight ahead and didn't glance back to see if their angelic little son had converted to misfit. If the window held out long enough, they'd never have to know.

Our little Dodge Omni, with its tires the size of small monochrome televisions, rolled over a pothole. The car jumped, I bounced in the backseat, and shards of glass rained down on me. At first it was only one or two, but soon the rest followed. They struck the awful grey plastic interior like a million little pin drops, and stuck to my woollen black tuque. Mother gasped and Father silently swiveled his ahead around. "What the fuck?" he said. He stopped the car, looked at the glass, looked at me, and then looked back at the glass. Then he turned the car around and gently drove home. At home, I bolted to my room and didn't come out until dinner.

Nick and I are near the sandpit in our school's playground rifling through our trading cards, trying to brag about worthy cards we have because of luck. This is Grade 6, I think. You can buy packs of eleven of these trading cards from grocery stores. They're stuffed in the same silvery packs that potato chips come in and hang right next to the gum racks, gossip magazines, and Archie comic books. The idea is that parents will bring their children grocery shopping, and as they wait for what is always too long a time at the cashier, their kids will beg for the colourful little pack of harmless trading cards. The cards are so cheap, it seems like an easy pacifier to plop in the kid's mouth.

So Nick and I are delving into our ownership addiction when Nick notices a card in my deck that he wants and I notice a card in his neck that I want. I propose a simple trade. Nick says no, says something about his card being more worthy than mine, and a simple trade would mean he's getting the shorter end of the stick. I'm a rather thick kid that believes my fellow human beings have immutable trustworthiness, so I ask Nick what he wants to do. It's a bad principle to hold onto in school.

Nick tells me we'll have to do a more complex trade. He says he'll give me the one card I want, I will give him both cards plus two lesser cards, and then he'll give me back the one card I want. I agree, and hesitantly make the switch. When we finish the trade, he gives me back the two lesser cards and keeps both good ones. "Ha!" he yells.

"Hey! Douche bag!" I shout back. Nick runs, I trail. "That's not fair! Give me my card."

"Nope."

"You twicked me!"

"I twicked you?" he replies. "Sure, I admit, I twicked you, whatever the hell that means. No, I don't know what you mean, speak normal. You're not retarded, right?"

"Give me my card."

"You didn't answer me," he says. "You're not retarded, right? Are you?"

"No, I'm not. I'm smart," I say.

"Some retarded people are smart, like that guy in the wheelchair," he says. "Or as you would call them: wetards."

"Will you stop!" I say. "I said you tw ... tw ... tricked me." Nick pauses. "So what?"

I stop, not really knowing what I will do if I do catch him. I'm not a violent person, so I don't do anything and the only way to get anything done on the playground is either be violent or be crafty. Nick is both.

Me, Nick, and Bob are near the dumpster behind the school eating microwave popcorn. We take turns shoving our grimy little hands into the buttery bag and pulling out fistfuls of white butterflies. School ended a while ago and the sun is beginning to set. We watch the janitors go back and forth in the school windows, and the eye-tired teachers finally making it to their cars. We throw the empty popcorn bag over our heads into the dumpster. Nick drops to a knee, opens his crummy backpack, and pulls out two items: the first another bag of microwave popcorn which he hands to Bob, and the second a canister of hairspray.

"Nick, I hate cold popcorn," Bob says. "Why don't we just go back to your place and make fresh stuff instead of stuffing it in your pack?"

"Don't be such a beef curtain," Nick says. "My brother's being a major nutsack at the moment and mom's gone for the week."

"What's with the hairspray?" I ask.

"Look, there's Pete," Nick says, pointing to the janitor in the window. "That's Aaron's dad. I fuckin' hate Aaron."

"Who's Aaron?" Bob asks.

"He's the one allergic to nuts," Nick says, "except for men's nuts."

"What?"

"I think I should come to class with a necklace of nuts around my neck, " Nick continues, "like a necklace of garlic to stop vampires. Every time Aaron comes around me I'll just shove my necklace of nuts in his face."

"Won't that kill him?"

"No," Nick says. "Or I don't know, how allergic can one be to nuts?"

"I'm not allergic to anything," Bob says, passing the popcorn bag to me.

I'm tired of eating popcorn and pass the bag to Nick. Nick thrusts his fist into the bag and pulls out the dead white butterflies. They crawl across his hand and fall to the ground, shriveling in the little pockets of moisture that dot the pavement around the dumpster. "What's the hairspray for?" I ask.

"I stole it from my sister," Nick says. "I want to try something."

He drops the bag of popcorn, still half-full, onto the ground beside the dumpster. He tells Bob and me to come in close. He pulls a box of matches from his pocket, leans down on the ground, lights a match, takes the canister of hairspray and sprays the match. Flames eat the spray and ignite the air with a wonderful orange glow. The colour seems so welcoming compared to the greyish palette that surrounds us. Nick smirks at Bob and me, licking his lip and bobbing his head.

"Cool, huh?" he says, delighted.

He pulls out another match and ignites his welfare flamethrower a second time. Little bits of flame spatter the metal dumpster and hiss into trails of smoke. Nick lights a third match and sprays. I can see the butter on his hands glisten under the flame's light. The flame eats its way through the spray, jumps past the canister, and lights Nick's hand on fire. The concoction of butter and trace amounts of arm hair singe. Nick jumps back and waves his arm around. Bits of hot, burning butter flick from his arm and hit Bob in the face. Bob cries out, slaps himself in the face, pulls up his shirt and rubs his cheeks in the shaggy fabric. Nick's arm was only on fire for a split second. He furiously looks over his arm before noticing that the bag of popcorn has caught fire. The flames are huge and lick at the dumpster's metal hull filled with eraser ends, old school assignments, school lunches, report cards, vomit, and construction paper chains of people holding hands in unity. Nick rushes over and stomps at the fire until it's out, until the air smells like burnt butter and popcorn. He stuffs the hairspray into his backpack and tells us to get out of here. Nick kicks the ashes of the dead butterflies underneath the dumpster and we walk home our separate ways.

★

The school is in the shape of a rectangle. The two shortest sides point east and west, and the longest sides point north and south. The west side overlooks a gravel parking lot offlimits to students. The east side has one huge rectangular window divided into four equal panes that overlook an asphalt courtyard, a sort of outdoor lobby space before the grassy baseball diamond and fractured basketball court. The huge window is rather high up on the wall. Only the yellow stained ceiling inside is visible from the courtyard.

I'm sitting on the ground with my back against the curled steel of the playground's fence when Nick and Bob finally arrive. Bob is lobbing a tennis ball up and down in the air. Nick is carrying three lacrosse sticks. The little netted pockets sprouting from one end of the stick look like the crotch cups football players shove down their pants.

I run over to the centre of the asphalt courtyard where Nick tosses me a lacrosse stick. "Are we still going to play Wall Ball?" I ask.

"It's called Red Ass," Nick says. "And yes we are. I thought we'd just take it up a notch."

"Where'd you get these?"

"I stole 'em," he says, "from my brother."

Nick snatches the tennis ball, places it in his stick's basket and whips it at the wall. It thuds against the brick and bounces back with diminished velocity.

"Why is it called Wed Ass?" I ask. "I thought it was always called Wall Ball."

"It's not *Wed* Ass—and only fairies call it Wall Ball," Nick says. "It's called Red Ass. If the ball hits the ground before it hits the wall or if you drop the ball, you have to go up face first to the wall, drop your pants, and one of us gets three tries whipping it at your ass."

"I don't want to do that," I say.

"Those the rules."

"Can't we just have fun?"

"Are you ready?" Nick asks.

We each grab a lacrosse stick and Nick whips the ball at the wall. The fuzzy orb blemished with manila-like stitching impacts the brick and flutters back, splashes in a puddle of yesterday's rain and lands in my basket. The pockmarked vowel retraces its trajectory from my net to the wall, hits the three-storey brick hedge with a faint drawing of moisture, bounces once and lands in Bob's basket. Bob lobs the ball towards the partition. It sputters on the ground and rolls into the junction between building and Earth, a failure of gravity to react in a way Bob has intended.

"Get to the wall, Bob," Nick says.

Bob nervously cups the tennis ball in his lacrosse basket and throws it back at the wall, hoping a do-over will erase any memory of the fact he failed the first time. Nick's memory isn't something anyone recognizes as tactful, but he isn't a potted plant.

"Get to the wall, Bob," Nick repeats.

Bob looks to me, his lower lip migrating away from his upper lip. I can see him getting trapped as he contemplates the rules of the game. He's trying to find an airhole, a flaw, a fluke that he can wiggle through. The rules seem so impenetrable, though—shut and nailed by logic.

"It was my first time," Bob says. "Give me a freebie and let's try again."

"No."

"If I screw up again, then I'll go to the wall," Bob says.

"That's not fair," Nick says.

"Why?"

"If me or Xavier had screwed up first, would you have given us a freebie?"

"Definitely," Bob says. Sweat snowballs down his forehead.

"You're lying," Nick says. "The rules are the rules."

"Why are the rules that way?" Bob asks. "They're our rules, we can change them to whatever we want."

"You just don't get it," Nick says. "Get to the wall, or you're no fun."

"I'm fun, I just want another chance," Bob says.

"Can we play alweady?" I ask.

"Get the cheater here to follow the rules then," Nick says.

I look to Bob. I sigh a heavy sigh, shrug my shoulders, try to express on my face the fact I don't want to argue with Nick. Bob would be a bad hostage. I walk in circles waiting for him to realize I want him to get it over with.

"I'll go to the wall if Xavier gets to shoot the ball," Bob negotiates.

Nick keeps a straight face, thinks for a minute. He clearly doesn't want to do this but seems unable to find a part of the Wall Ball constitution that denies this as an option. Bob throws me the ball and runs to the wall.

"Don't be a girl and pretend to throw hard," Nick says to me. He looks at me as if he is trying to search my heart for the on/off switch to my aortic valve.

I wish Bob had negotiated this comprise with me beforehand, as much as it's a good idea. What do I do, though? Do I attempt my best impression of Cy Young with a lacrosse stick and hope Nick is fooled? Or do I respect the rules of the game and actually try hard to hit Bob square on the ass, hoping that I simply miss? Hoping physics isn't as predictable as I think it is? Bob seems confident that whatever I do, it will not result in his ass blushing red. He seems confident that whatever I do will not get him hurt. He is surely more confident than I am.

Bob drops his pants slightly, his hands holding his belt so that they don't fall down any further. I take one quick glance of a target I have no desire to study and throw the ball, my psyche still bouncing between how I should go about this. In my over thinking, as the ball is released from the basket and traverses the air, I realize just how much energy has streamed through my arm, transferred to the lacrosse stick, and infused the tennis ball with velocity. I don't hear the typical, vibrating wallop of a ball hitting a brick wall. Instead, I hear a peculiar, deflated thud—followed by Bob screaming. Tears are instantly recognizable on his face. He pulls up his pants faster than the time it took for the ball to go from the basket to his ass and runs home.

Nick walks over to the spot Bob made his error and picks up his lacrosse stick. "Don't worry about him," he says. "He'll get over it by recess tomorrow."

"Are you going to say sorry to him?" I ask.

"Don't be stupid, people don't actually apologize for things," he says.

"My parents say sorry to each other all the time," I say.

"I'm going home," Nick says, and snatches the last lacrosse stick from my hands.

CHAPTER 7: HIGH SCHOOL

Grade 12. A fog was settling in to disorient migrating mallards, ducks, other parasitic birds as I stood outside the high school's front doors after school. The low cloud cover formed an infinite sense of enclosure, a comforting claustrophobia. The world had shrunk. The pillows of moisture pervading the air provided a cushy cage to the day's offering of time. This is how I met Felix. We were attending an ad hoc political candidate's rally. We stood near the entrance waiting to see who was running for some ineffectual municipal office. Other students streamed by heading for yellow bricks to brisk them over potholes and crosswalks straight to pizza pockets and the early stages of internet porn. I had my own political ambitions and thought that regardless of what fringe candidate would take to the sidewalk curb, this was good networking on my part.

Political rallies, like protests, feel very much like circuses, that sort of freakish moment of history that stings a burning question into the back of the brain cavity: what the hell have we gotten ourselves into? Seeing a circus elephant twirl its tricks—a feat for our immature amusement that no doubt requires exhaustive use of the creature's tiny brain—brings about a similar reaction one has upon hearing a loudmouthed callous wannabe call his political opponent a communist. As soon as silence descends, the weight of reality rushes in with similar force to the invisible pull of gravity. It digs deep. It turns infectious. Suddenly the subtle plan of a capitalist society driven by the lines of a calendar become all too clear—a shocking, dystopian, dislodging disclosure that this is all there is and is ever going to be. No fancy car or friend can change that. Sure, hiding out in the woods is one way to escape the very core of our hallway culture, but is eluding the entrapment of cyclical materialism and consumption really worth it if your chances of becoming a moose's fuck buddy are increased?

Fringe candidates seem not the least bit at odds with this cynicism. Actually, I'm sure it's their main source of protein. That and racism.

Anyway, on a dreary Monday, a political candidate in a municipal election was outside our high school attempting to woo a crowd of students only one-tenth of whom were legally allowed to vote. The candidate, Mr. Tancredo, the Vanman (the man with a minivan), who was an employee of some sort at our school. I really don't remember what he did. He could have been a student for all I knew. Mr. Tancredo was a remarkably unforgettable figure for looking so unremarkable. He was white, and that was about the only discernable quality he had. He could get lost in a crowd of two people. He was a nice, genuine man who had two unfortunate qualities: first, when he stopped talking, it appeared his brain had shut off, and second, he was a warped new age religious nutcase. Mr. Tancredo was very much a dangerous mix of Santa Claus jolliness and conspiracy theories. Yet this attitude never got him fired from our school. On the contrary, he had abruptly left just so he could run in the election. The school and PTA expended most of its outrage on knives and guns being brought to school by students instead. This is also the reason old Mr. Vanman was allowed to hold his impromptu speaking sessions on the school's parking lot under the trunk door of his minivan, which was plastered with homemade political posters.

Usually people like Mr. Tancredo found themselves with microphones in their faces, their fringe thinking a deliciously wrapped chocolate bar of sensationalism. Alas, not for Mr. Vanman. There were fewer than six of us on that cloudy day, most of us attending for our own selfish purposes. I was there to further a fledgling political career, two others were from the school newspaper, and Felix was waiting for his mother. It was immediately clear Mr. Tancredo's claim of being part of a refreshing soda pop-sounding new age religion was really just a cover for his own demented take on just about every major spirituality. For something that sounded so fantastically complex when the man talked of it himself—a post-post-modern religion for a waning post-modern society—a quick reflection of his views appeared to show a religion as multi-dimensional as a sewer grate. At first it was an attractive prospect, but soon the attractiveness dwindled when Mr. Tancredo attempted to use it as a viable springboard for his political decisions.

Whatever happened to the separation of church and lunacy?

In a way, Mr. Tancredo could have been smarter than he appeared, attempting to get the jump on humanity's eventual realization that religion is as compliant and easy to swallow as Lego and lead-based paint; that eventually, as globalization becomes ever more inevitable, the transfer of knowledge and ideas ultimately affecting the doctrines of our sacred religions, they will cross over each other in a slow and tortuous merger of tradition and modern thinking.

I'd like to think he was just a nutcase.

"Any questions?" Mr. Tancredo asked.

"Do you have any pot?" someone asked, predictably.

"No, but I have money for it."

"Really?"

"No."

I would've believed in Santa Claus if he gave out pot.

"Dude, this guy's insane," the boy standing next to me whispered.

I looked over. I had seen him before on our school's soccer team (and I only remember this from the unfortunate fact that the team was atrocious. They didn't appear to know what sport they were playing. Their lack of strategy might have better suited them to playing ping-pong).

"Hey," I responded, "I know you. You're on our awful soccer team."

Felix glared at me. "Well, that's not my fault," he said. "Aren't you our former terrible Grade 12 representative on that pompous student panel?"

"Uh . . ."

"The representative who called all his opponents 'fascist sympathizers'?"

"Well . . . sort . . . I don't know about this guy," I said, quickly changing the subject.

"You don't think he's a lunatic?"

"I don't know, he's trying pretty hard to be a lunatic. Maybe we're missing something."

"He's a classic brokerage politician."

"A classic what?"

"He's a pretentious nobody. He thinks he can pander to every major religion and ethnic group by claiming to believe in just about everyone's religion."

"Oh, it's intentional?" I asked. "I guess that makes more sense. I was going to say his brain waves don't seem so far off from a doorknob's, but your theory sounds better."

"I'm not joking."

"Neither was I."

"It's not admirable. He's a regular pandering politician with a forgettable education in rock climbing or something."

"Come on. He's so jolly, like Santa Claus."

"Santa Claus is a panderer too. That's probably where politicians get their inspiration."

"You've destroyed my childhood," I said. "Don't vote for him then."

"Well, I'm not going to. And I can't anyway," Felix said. "But if others believe this nonsense—"

"I wouldn't think much of it. If these are the types of people he attracts, he's going to go as far as the liquor store."

"Come on, guys, I'm open to everyone's opinion," Mr. Tancredo continued. "Let's have a conversation. Speak up."

"Why not tell him what you think?" I asked, turning to Felix.

"Okay, fine," Felix said. "Watch what happens." He raised his hand. "Sir?"

Mr. Tancredo pointed with a smile. "Yes, you."

"This isn't really much of a question, but I think you're a lunatic," Felix said.

"Well, isn't it great we live in a country where you can say that," Mr. Vanman replied, unflinchingly.

"Why wouldn't I be able to say it in any other country? Wouldn't you have to be elected first?"

"You have the right to free speech."

"I'm not saying it because I have the right to."

"Okay, son, that's great," Mr. Vanman said. "Are you even old enough to vote?"

"You said you wanted a conversation, did you not?"

"Any other questions or comments?" The Vanman had had enough. Felix seemed agitated. "Come on, tell me about your aspirations for life, tell me about the sort of career you want to have after high school. I'll tell you why those greedy fat cats are trying to stop you from achieving it and how I can change that if elected. How about you?" he asked, pointing at me.

"Me?" I said.

"Yes. Anything?"

"I want to become Prime Minister."

There was silence, then stares, confusion, cackles and scorn. It was dramatic stillness, given the beige wallpaper environment of a high school parking lot. The expressions mirrored the dreary straight faces people show as they search for a thought with their sarcasm alarms set to full power.

"You're all jealous, I know," I said.

"Why would you want to become Prime Minister?" asked one of the potheads.

"That's like wanting to become a circus director or a principal," added another.

"Yeah," Mr. Tancredo said, "I mean wow. I don't even care to become a member of parliament. Hell, I don't even care to become a city councillor."

"Then why are you in our high school's parking lot holding a political rally?" Felix said. "For people who can't even vote nonetheless."

"I'm just trying to get attention," Mr. Tancredo answered. "Maybe if I'm enough of a loudmouth or a nuisance, the city will place me somewhere else. Like the school board or maybe the sanitation department."

"What about all that new age religion stuff?"

"What? Oh, I don't know. It doesn't matter," Mr. Tancredo said. "It's just language, son. If you play your cards right, language can get you far."

"That's pretty pathetic."

"Good advice," I said.

"Dude, don't listen to him," Felix warned.

"Get with the times, son," Mr. Tancredo said. "I may be an old crackpot to you guys, but I'm a self-aware crackpot."

"If you're self-aware, why not just stop being a crackpot?"

"Take it from me," Mr. Tancredo continued, ignoring him, "if you want to succeed, refining your ideas is a waste of time. Refining your words, saying the right thing, now that will get you far."

We were all a little dumbstruck. "But won't that make us empty shells, hollow minds, stuff like that," I asked.

"Well . . . yeah," Mr. Tancredo hesitated, "but what's wrong with that? None of us are going to be remembered anyway."

"Why not?"

"Because no one cares," Mr. Tancredo said. "Everyone's too busy refining their own languages. Self-absorption is a terribly fun disease, let me tell you."

"That's disgusting," Felix said.

"I didn't make up the rules," Mr. Tancredo replied, "or reality. I mean all we've been doing so far is discussing language. It's all around us." We all looked around us. "Which one of you wanted to be Prime Minister?"

"What's wrong with a little ambition," I sputtered, chuckling.

"But why Prime Minister?"

"Why not?"

"They get pies thrown in their faces," a pothead remarked.

"And doused in chocolate milk," remarked another pothead.

"So what?"

"Why not be ambitious for something with real power?" Mr. Tancredo said, "like a bank executive. That way you get to be hated by the general public without being so obvious. It's a win-win."

"I don't want it for the power."

"Really."

"I don't really know why I want it," I said, thinking. "I'd just love to have those little desk headers that read 'Prime Minister of Canada.' Those are slick. There's also some people I'd like to get back at, rub their faces in the fact that I could deport them on the spot to some place really pathetic. Like Disney World."

"Revenge, of course," Mr. Tancredo said. "Good to see it's still strong in the youngsters."

"We're not youngsters," I coughed.

"No one is finding this sickening?" Felix said, shouting, surprised.

"What do you mean?"

"This is all bullshit," he said. "It's just generalizations. It's a recipe for a hollow and unfulfilling life."

Mr. Tancredo looked offended. "And? What exactly is the alternative?"

Felix stuttered, "I don't know. Happiness?"

"I'm happy," Mr. Tancredo said. "A lot of people like me are happy. You see the problem is you think that people fall from cheery goodness and happiness into being nameless idiots. It's the other way around."

"That's pretty cynical."

"So?" Mr. Tancredo said, childishly. "It doesn't change anything. People can still have ambition. It's just an ambition to escape. That's all. Nothing wrong with that."

"I don't think so," Felix persisted. "You're a classic new age religious nut who probably believes libraries count as excessive government intrusion in society. You're the last person to listen to."

"But the first to get attention," Mr. Tancredo noted.

"Whatever."

"Well, this was fun," Mr. Tancredo said, smiling. He started packing up. "But I must leave you because I have to go and volunteer at a soup kitchen tonight."

"Pandering to the poor takes up time, doesn't it?"

"You betcha."

The potheads walked off in a cloud of indecipherable gibberish. Mr. Tancredo got into his minivan and puttered off. Felix remained visibly agitated.

"He'd get more votes if he weren't such a depressing asshole," he said.

"I thought you didn't like him because he was a political hack," I said.

"That too. There's enough of him to hate to go around. The fat Santa bastard."

"You stayed, you talked."

"Why did you let him shred your ambitions like that?" Felix said, turning to me.

"Everyone does that."

"And you're fine with it?"

"I ask them what they want to do when they grow up," I replied, "then make fun of them for picking something underpaid or trailer trashish or whatever."

"Well, that's certainly an aggressive defence."

"I could make fun of anyone's ambition."

"How about musician?" Felix asked.

"Pretentious nutjob," I said, "no need for music anyway."

"Actor?"

"Egotistical trash."

"Teacher?"

"Underpaid monotony."

"Priest, minister, cleric?"

"Well, who the hell would want that?" I said. Felix shrugged his shoulders, looked around the parking lot. "Waiting for something?" I asked.

"Ride. Need one?" he asked. "Mom's got a minivan."

"I could use a ride. Where do you live?"

"Close by."

"Sure."

"There she is." Felix waved like a matador. Maybe his mother was half blind, in which case I didn't want to be in her minivan.

The minivan morphed into view in a streak of green. It circled around our potholed parking lot as a lumbering testament to banality, and as family friendly essential as drugs are to the Medellín Cartel. On the bumper were stickers: a sideways silver "We Support the Troops", and a "My Son's an Honour Student".

The tombstone with wheels screeched to a halt in front of us, nearly running over my foot. Felix with a fair bit of finesse fiddled with the sliding door, pulling and pushing what appeared to have been meant for a freezer. I climbed in with no sense of dignity, strapped on the seatbelt with a click. Felix smashed the door shut scaring the shit out of me. He got around to the front seat.

"Hi there, who's this?" Felix's mother asked.

"Mom, this is Xavier," Felix answered, announcing me as if he were an after dinner speaker.

"Hello, Xavier. I'm Liana," Felix's mother said.

Liana could best be described by two words: plump and aging. Her rapid ascent to the age of 50 or so was blatantly apparent. She had short, shoulder length, platinum blonde hair that, under the right light, appeared ash. She was as natural and untouched as the day she was born.

"Is this a new buddy, Felix?" Liana asked.

Her voice was shrill. Maybe she did Disney animation voiceovers as a pastime or had spent her life talking down to household pets. It was all so very cheery.

"Nice to meet you, Liana," I said.

"Oh, that's okay; you can call me Mom."

"Excuse me?"

"Everyone does," she giggled. It was a genuine giggle.

I looked to Felix for confirmation. He was smiling, unmoved. Her heartfelt warmth could boil water faster than a stove. Felix revelled in her; in fact, to my surprise, he was the furthest thing from embarrassed. For me, I'm rarely to be found in the same car as my parents, let alone found having a conversation with them.

"So, Mr. Xavier. What did you say your last name was?" Liana asked.

"Bernard."

"Bernard? Oui?" she said, lighting up. "Parlez-vous français?"

"What?"

"Bernard. That's French. You speak French?" she repeated in French, I think.

"Oh, sorry, no. Are you guys bilingual?" I asked.

"Only Mother is," said Felix, proudly.

"I took French Immersion in high school," Liana said. "It's wonderful to know. You kids should think about learning it."

"It would certainly help me get a job," I said. "Is that why you know it?"

Liana and Felix giggled. "Oh, I don't have a job," she smiled, brightly, proudly, almost with a whiff of superiority. I'm a home-maker."

"You build homes?"

"I stay at home and run errands and take care of things and . . . well, you must be familiar with homemakers, no? What does your mother do?"

"My mother? She does something at a daycare or a nursery school or something. She could be going off every morning and raising hamsters for all I know," I said.

"That's unfortunate. It's too bad your mother works."

I paused to think that through. "What?" I said.

"Xavier here is Grade 12 representative, or he was, at least," Felix blurted. "He wants to become Prime Minister."

"Oooooo . . ." Liana turned around to smile brightly at me, which was terrifying because she was also driving. I could only smile back, grip the seat, hope Felix could look past the cheery triviality and object in order to save our lives. "That's very cool," she continued, turning back around. "What made you want to be Prime Minister?"

I had to think for a minute, censoring the real reason. "Just a strong desire to apply my values and help Canadians."

"That's so great."

I paused. "Yes."

No. Here's the real reason.

Growing up in Slanty McGee with bad parents made the world worryingly unfair for an impressionable youth like myself. As police arrived to investigate our stolen stereo, Father would be rambling about a New World Order having arrived to shut him up. Our lives were all made worse by further dis-repairs: fire hazards, schizophrenic one-way streets, stupid neighbours, shoddy porches that city engineers left imbedded with a bus, turning our home into a tourist attraction. One side of the bus sported the atheist ad; the other side had a political campaign poster for a Prime Minister seeking re-election, his grinning face surrounded by a grey-haired halo. All of these things accumulated as a wound, a scar, a shattered experience. Certainly things could have been worse, but things could have also always been a whole lot better. Whitey McConcrete and its unmoving rawness—dissatisfaction and misrepresentation—were all we had. There was anger, there was passion, and there was this indelible memory floating in front of my face of a bus ad with a flat-faced smiling Prime Minister pledging tax cuts in order to cut social assistance for people like us. If being at the top meant being an easy target, then fine. My hate was going to help me achieve all the revenge I needed. Those theories swirling in my head passed down from Father about government conspiracies and big brother always watching made it tantalizing for me to think that I could be that person instilling fear in others. I decided to start on my journey to achieve this position early on.

In grade school I was ambitious, proud, ignorant, all the calling cards of a dedicated politician. Like any energized egotist I knew, I would succeed in carrying out my poorly thought out thoughts, mainly because I happened to be one of the few who was actually committed. I became the Grade 6, 7, and 8 representative for student council partially because of my intrepid integrity, but mostly because I was the only one to show up. On the voting ballot, however, my name didn't numerically appear as a majority despite my unbeatable position of being the only candidate. Most simply penned in things like "That kid that feeds the hamster" or "worm-eater."

At first, the seemingly incurable power vacuum wrought onto the student body (a result of the fact that the student body didn't have any power to begin with) was difficult to deal with given my plan for wrath and revenge and all. Power was earned, I knew, and so I soldiered on.

I ravaged my resume with cheap political rewards, namely representative for student council from grades 6 through 12, calling these achievements "major learning experiences". My asinine addresses to student body-sponsored events riveted the crowds in classroom and assembly alike. If stoned or smashed enough, the student herd shovelled down and soaked in my nicely worded non-sequiturs, sexual innuendos, and other rhetorical slush. I was made for the job, nurtured by the false sense of power it gave me. Just look at this speech I once gave. I didn't even have to plagiarize anyone that important:

"In your eyes, I'm nothing but a political parasite, a blood sucking creature shouting about meaningless numbers, lamenting false compassion, describing misconstrued empathy. But today, I stand before you working, moving, progressing, fighting for whatever you need, require, desire. I cannot tell you what you want or what you need. I'm not here to speak for you or make decisions for you. I'm here to represent you, to lead you towards those goals. Join me! Vote for me! And you will damn well know after marking that X next to my name that you've chosen the right candidate for the job and the right future!"

My anonymous detractors suggested afterward that my speech was unrealistically broad and unspecific. I was a candidate who took a meagre high school apolitical election way too seriously. My response was childish, rude, raw, and largely arrogant, but it was no less profound: "I'll never back down!" Polemical wallabies. It was falsely empowering. It felt great.

Back when I was riding in Liana's minivan, I had already lost my Grade 12 student representative position because one mild day, an athletics coach the size of two beach balls glued together caught me smoking on school property with members of the unbelievably incompetent soccer team. The coach nearly went into cardiac arrest when he laid eyes on his laughably bad athletes lighting up. Logical reasoning didn't persuade the coach to believe my account, that it was really just a "meet and greet" with cigarettes as a proxy for the ever awkward "Hello, how are you today?" It was a social circle absent of invitations where others were responsible for their own drugs and inevitable endings. It wasn't my fault his athletes were smokers or idiots or both.

Coach didn't care.

When I first saw the fat tub of lard lumbering over like an oversized stick of butter on stilts, I couldn't imagine a consequence from my harmlessly conversing with some moronic acquaintances. "What the hell are you doing?" he yelled.

"Knitting," I said.

I'd meant to say nothing, but the cough perverted the sound. We bribed him with the two tall cans of beer and some cigarettes.

Some time later, on a different school day, I was called to the Principal's office and was informed I would be fired from student council.

"Why?" I asked.

"Well, we got a complaint from Coach the other day," the principal said, chewing gum, "and apparently he found you being a 'bad influence', as he writes, not only smoking but also committing the crime on school property no less."

I kept tight-lipped on the fact that I had shown up to class after lunch plastered out of my brain. "How gaspingly reproachable," I said, with an innocent chuckle.

"Son, there's a fucking monstrous red sign over the front doors that says, 'For the love of Jesus don't smoke on school property or we'll be getting city fines far up the ass," the principal continued. "Don't tell me you didn't see it?"

"Mr. Turdidson—"

"It's Turgidson."

"Do you even have the power to fire me?" I asked.

"No."

"Right," I said, "so . . . I'm not leaving."

"No, we're firing you one way or the other," he said. "How about you just get the hell out of my office and be thankful I'm firing you. I could also try and find a way to kick your ass out onto the curb."

I didn't know what to make of it. I would find out later, well after graduation, that the soccer team, in an effort to avoid punishment from their butter-eating fat sack of crap coach, proclaimed that I had persuaded them to smoke. I had been their scapegoat.

That wasn't going to be the end of my dream, though. To fill my time and add to my resume, I became a youth volunteer at several obscure political offices for slightly below obscure politicians, like that of Careen Poxi, a narcissistic 10-time municipal mayoral candidate (running for mayor in more than one place) who had also been given the record of most attempted hate-crime indictments. Turns out that repeating that claim through a continuous loop of radio and television ads wasn't such a smart idea. After she was run out of town, I held a similarly obscure unpaid position for John "the Don" Mancha, who frequently found himself the target of flying Miguel De Cervantes novels thrown by opponents.

Back in the minivan, I was questioning the species in front of me. Who were these strangers, these strange subscribers to successful conformity, these people with paradoxical personalities and skills driving me home, offering me a ride, reviewing my life?

Felix lived on the edge of an unofficial suburb bordering that invisible barrier between Scarborough and Toronto. It was dreadfully boring on this side of the universe. I felt unhinged when I saw their home, almost a sickness of the stomach. It was large but not humongous, homogeneous but impersonal. It was a terrifyingly cute home. It had a car garage, a second floor, a front yard, a back yard, presumably a power lawn mower, other unnecessary necessities. It was white, black trimmed, with a black gate and black lettering that read *The Clarksons* in cursive writing, missing an apostrophe. Lawn: crisp. Driveway: sparkling. Windows: transparent. Dimensions: perfect. Me: vomiting. What we had here was a living space as exceptional as a four-point intersection. It was as Canadian as it was American. It had a doormat. It read "Go to Hell," I think.

The minivan mulled over the barely nullified hump introducing the driveway and garage, a whitewashed barn nearly identical in size to my future apartment. The garage door folded up with mystical precision.

"I'd hate to end our conversation here," Liana said, parking. "Why don't you come inside, meet the Clarkson clan."

I hesitated.

★

I'm asleep in the passenger seat of Felix's broken Jaguar when a forceful thud in my lap wakes me from my uncomfortable slumber. I snort and see my manuscript sprawled across my thighs.

"Look at this," Felix says, pointing to my manuscript.

I rub my eyes and stall for time, adjusting my seat unnecessarily before I looked it over. "I don't understand," I say. "What's the problem?"

"I know what you're doing. Don't think I don't know what you're doing."

"What am I doing?"

"You're trying to be a dramatic dullard," he says. "Trying to make an otherwise boring situation into something suspenseful. That shit ain't going to work when you're talking about someone's lawn. Lawn isn't exciting."

"Some people find it exciting," I say.

"Shut up and look at it."

"What? What am I suppose to be looking at? What have I done?"

"Look what's missing."

I read through my pithy paragraphs, note Felix's pen markings, chuckle at my own sense of humour, and finally see what Felix is on about. "Don't worry about that, I've given enough clues. They can figure it out."

"Why?" he asks.

"Because readers are not vegetables?"

"No, I mean why even do it that way?"

"Because it's chronological. I'm trying to make it unfold for the reader the same way it unfolded for me," I say.

"So you can see into the future?" he says. I shrug, innocently. "Chronological?" he continues. "This thing is like *Pulp Fiction* minus everything good about *Pulp Fiction*."

"Movie or book genre?"

"Don't play dumb."

I hand back the manuscript. "Is that your only problem so far?" I ask. "Just keep reading."

★

"Sure," I said, hesitantly, stepping out of the minivan.

Their garage was lush with labelled clear plastic bins filled with various spectrums of items. It was like looking into the not too distant future, the future being something a couple of years ago.

We made our way around the front, the garage door folding down behind us with the same whiff of undignified power as when it had gone up.

Once inside, we were submerged in a sea of greyish blue. It was a drink of warm water. It was almost overwhelming. I initially mistook the interior as hallway plastered in white sheets of plain paper. The carpet was so grey, so banal, it robbed a person of his energy. Everything seemed narrow. Everything seemed perfectly placed. Was I in a church? I don't think there's any way to get around just how plain the Clarkson home was. Even the word "plain" or comparing it to a mailing envelope would be too eccentric to apply to their home.

The floor plan was as predictable as a folding chair. A lanky hallway greeted the door, serviced by a stupidly placed shoe closet behind its hinges. A few paces forward was the gleaming Clarkson kitchen with its cascade of white tiles, teacups, tables, tinkling home appliances, titillating cupboards, counter tops bathed in blue marble. It was postcard approved, tough yet timid. A golf ball coloured colossal fridge—breaking the blue marble flow—was infected with fridge photographs, postcards, magnets, all proclaiming some sort of pathetic pun. "Is your refrigerator running . . ." read one. "Wok on the wild side," read another. "An apple a day is redundant because you'll burn in hell either way," read the last.

I might have misread that one though.

Felix's jolly father appeared before me. This man was closer to the roundness of a beach ball than an actual beach ball. He was taller than all of us, but barely. He had a handsomely floppy face, white hair, wrinkles, slightly tanned skin, a checkered short-sleeved button-down shirt tucked into beige dress pants, golden watch on his right wrist. A chiselled chin poked beneath the flab.

"Who's this young fella?" Felix's father asked, patting my shoulder and shaking my hand simultaneously. "Bobby Clarkson, how you doing?"

He was a full-fledged John Madden impersonator at that point. "I'm . . . exceptional," I spat, gulped, felt uneasy. "Are you a sports announcer?"

Bobby chortled like a stuffed vacuum. "No, no, son," he said, still shaking my hand. "I'm a book publisher, actually. I work at William & William Publishing. Must have heard of them, Canada's largest publisher of popular fiction. We got a lot of number one bestsellers under our belt. Will you be joining us for dinner . . . uh . . . ?"

"Xavier."

"Xavier, of course," he said. Liana walked off into the kitchen mist. I smelt roast.

"I don't know yet," I said.

"Wait, it's 'Xavier'?" Bobby asked. "You wouldn't happen to have been named after St. Francis Xavier, would you?"

"Who?"

"Dinner's on. Will you be joining us, Mr. Bernard?" Liana spoke suddenly.

"What? Oh, well, I don't know," I answered.

"Come, if you're a friend of Felix's, you're a friend of ours. We'd love to get to know you," Bobby bellowed, lumbering over the creaking kitchen tiles.

Felix followed. I followed Felix. Across from the kitchen in the farthest end of the house was a large living room. For a book publisher's house, it was astonishing how few books I had seen so far. I saw a cook book.

"I know it's a bit early," Liana said, placing a roast on their golden dinner table, "but it's not every day we have company."

I had lost all control to the most un-controlling. These people couldn't park a car if they had the steering wheel in their hands. "I guess it couldn't hurt," I stuttered, reviewing the red roast. "Could I just use your phone?"

"As long as you're not calling Russia," Bobby chortled, and his stomach undulated like a trampoline bearing too many kids. "It's in the living room, go right ahead."

I walked over. Their living room was decorated decisively. I picked up the phone, fastidiously placed next to a three-piece sofa set in matching black leather. Opposite, up against a wall, stood a massive credenza populated with an ostentatiously large television, stereo system, video player, and other gizmos. The other view of the outside world was a tiny rectangular window that merely looked into a hedge.

I was about to dial when I looked up. A repulsively large replication of Leonardo De Vinci's *Last Supper* hung above their sofa. I gulped, took a second glance around. On their matching coffee table was a golden trimmed Bible and above the doorway hung a golden cross.

The Clarksons were committed Christians.

I put the phone back down, walked back to the kitchen.

I was surrounded not by people, not by the masses, not by the tantalizing physique of grape juice labelled 'red wine' or fluffy bread squares forming a pyramid on a silver plate, ready for me to steal, bathe in bleach and feed to seagulls. I was surrounded by written words, by scorched battle-hardened scripture as battered as a fleshless soldier stabbed and buried shortly after wasting his life in a barely recollected conflict.

I swallowed spit, swivelled my eyes, caressed the carpet with sock feet. I was at odds with the task this dinner had become. I had to keep my mouth shut. I would never have to see them again. I wouldn't have to ruin their dinner. We all seek to satisfy a desire for dignity, it's just that we disagree on what it means to be dignified. Then we insult, ridicule, and call each other ridiculous.

When I returned to the table two new people were seated with us: Felix's nine-year old sister Jessica and his twenty-one-year old brother Joseph. Jessica looked strikingly similar to Bobby, Joseph looked similar to Liana, and Felix appeared meekly related to them all. Jessica hadn't encountered the opportunity to be emotionally thwacked upside the head yet, so I'll skip her because she's boring. Joseph on the other hand was primed and ready for shocking documentary-style description and deadpan interpretive photography. He was the kind of guy who cut off ambulances. On registration forms he surely put "No, I am not" when asked for

Postal. He read as a non-conformist with a pretence of non-conformity, which cancelled the former out and made the latter so.

The dinner was itself quite intriguing. It was ritualistic, hierarchal, almost archaic in its set up. Bobby sat at one end of the rectangular table and Liana sat at the other end with the children snatching the last four available seats. Bobby sat first, spoke first, and ate first, but he did nothing. If something had to be placed or decorated, Liana was the one to get up and find it. Before I or anyone else could stab a fork in a potato, we had to hold the hand of the person beside us, close our eyes, and recite some sort of supernatural verse. Bobby, of course, was the one that led this ritual. After that, however, it was just like any other meal in a fast food restaurant. Liana would recognize misbehaviour from one of the children, and Bobby would be the enforcer, apart from the fact that the most talkative person at the table by the end of it was, without a doubt, innocent little Jessica, the only one at the table who had no idea of the parental imprint that would inevitably shut her up until adulthood, when her opportunity to swing the emotional-instability hammer down squarely onto her own offspring would come.

I awoke the day after the dinner fresh from a fuming bout of over-thinking on whom I had made connections with the night before. It's the sort of train of thought that feels substantial and poignant one second, but the next appears to have the same depth as a piece of liquorice. It's an oddly empty feeling, like a bucket of flies. In order to clear my head, I jumped onto some public transit and went downtown for a walk.

On my walk, I found Felix pretending to be friendly to random pedestrians while holding up a charity form, a clip board, and a punctual take on public solicitation. He had informed me of his employment the night before. It was one of his first paid opportunities and the only thing he detested was the pink shirt he had to wear. I met up with him to see how it was going, that being the non-suspicious thing to do.

I materialized before him. "Hello, sir, would you like to learn . . ." he began. "Oh, it's you. You found me."

"Having fun?" I asked.

"Plenty."

"Any sign-ups?"

"Thankfully no."

"No?"

"I don't feel like talking today."

"What charity?"

"The sick kids hospital up the street," he said. The same place that housed Kenny, Jesus of Narcissism.

A business man with a Blackberry appeared before us. "Sir," Felix shouted, "you look like a successful man. How would you like to donate a fraction of your wealth in order to help a . . ." The man passed by, wordless. "And a good day to you, sir, may you be impaled on the hood of the speeding ambulance carrying the child you could have helped save if only you had the personality to donate."

"What are you doing?" I said.

"The only people who sign up are cash-strapped hippies and university students," he said, rubbing his forehead. "Would you like to sign up?"

"I don't have a job."

"You wouldn't be the first," he said. "We are standing on land worth more than some countries, more than people's lives, and I still only get sign-ups from the passing hippies, mostly."

"How does that happen?"

"I don't know," he paused. A business woman was heading our way. "Madam, dying children would love for you to donate just a little . . ." She walked on by. "If not, I do predict you'll land face first in a gutter and drown amongst coffee cups and cell-phone cards," he yelled.

"Why don't you try and be nice to them?"

"Because then they'll just politely refuse to sign up," he said. "The way I do it, I get to fuck around with them, have some power over the people who are powerful."

"But you're making them feel guilty."

"Should I try a different emotion?" A young man was coming our way. "Sir," Felix yelled, ";how would you like to take your mind off your hideousness and donate to a children's charity. The money will help to . . ."

"He didn't even take a second glance," I said.

"Well, what are they going to do? Sue a charity?"

"So, you've gone from playing on people's guilt to playing on their insecurities."

"I actually get paid for this."

"But doesn't it hurt to see this?" I asked.

"Yes, it does, if I'm honest," he stuttered. "All these well-off rich people not giving a shit about the future we have to deal with. What's wrong with society?"

"Felix, I can tell you right now, everyone already knows what you're talking about," I said. "You're not the first to bring it up."

"Uh huh, and?"

"Growing up, you find out that what you think is new is already known," I continued, proudly. "And what isn't known is not obvious."

"Okay, fantastic. If everyone already knows it, why doesn't someone do something about it?" he asked.

I was without words. "I don't know."

"Ah ha! You see!" he shouted then laughed. "No one knows shit. No one! For the split seconds we, us, youth, whatever we're called, think about all this bullshit, we are the smartest people on this planet."

"I wouldn't go that far."

"I would. I am right now." He was getting excited. "This is why I'm here shouting at . . . hey, you . . . yeah, you . . . go fuck yourself. . . . See, they don't do anything. I love public solicitation. What a wonderful right we all have, eh?"

"Calm down. Try not to forget you're working for a charity."

"I never forget it," he said. "But to these people it's all just stupid language, honestly. Half the people who sign up just like to have bragging rights."

"Well, at least they're donating."

"You know what we should do?" he said. "We should give everyone—who hasn't experienced it of course—diabetes or cancer or some illness."

"Good idea. Donations will skyrocket once we kill off half the population."

"I don't think it would be that high, as long as you don't put me in charge."

"How long have you been at this?"

"It was just a theory," he said. "Why are you even out here? Are you a garbage collector?"

"I said I was unemployed."

"So you're just walking."

"Yeah."

"And? How's that going?"

"It's an underrated activity," I said.

"Got to love it," he said, and started dancing. "You know we're always looking for new people."

I left.

On Sunday afternoon I ran into Felix and his family at the mall. It began as a weekend window-shopping spree with Mother and Father. I noted long ago that the last people I would want or should spend time with was Mother and Father. But somehow I found myself a blind bird desperate for someone's shoulder, so I drudged along beside them.

The Sunday shoppers with nothing else to do were a menacing bunch, especially when enclosed together in a ventilated box. They wander like zombies for hours, maybe even worse than zombies because they don't know what they want.

I slumped along, failing to belong, navigating the floating morgue of worn clothes. Through this mist of fabric, I told my parents I'd meet them later and lunged into a t-shirt kiosk. I lost myself amongst t-shirt quotes, misquoted texts, misprinted pop culture icons with skewed colour arrangements from a bad printing press, Made in China stickers next to Canadian flags, and counterfeit wallets. It felt comforting to be pillowed between copyright infringements. I sauntered past the owner sitting in a plastic garden chair. He flicked off a piece of Lo Mein that had fallen on his Portuguese soccer jersey, stabbed at the rest of his Styrofoam food. I could hear his fresh can of vending machine soda fizzing in its aluminum tube. Shouted Hindi penetrated the weak t-shirt fabric hung on garden fencing. A man in denim overalls teetered on a silver ladder close to a burnt light, gesturing for his assistant to pass him a screwdriver. A little boy in a blue shirt crashed headfirst into a stranger's purse and fell to the ground, glared up at the face of an unknown.

I strolled out of the kiosks, biologically led by the scent of Food Court food. I paddled through traffic, dipping, diving, slipping past slack jawed semi-circles, baby carriages, gawking shocked tourists delighted and appalled at our collective mentality to stomach overpriced headphones, cellphone plans, fake jewellery. I bolted by a book store promoting moral interpretation. I glanced at a techno-gizmo store selling technologically-assisted common sense.

I reached the food court. The open plains of floating fried bacon, reheated under the skylights' scorching sun, filled the air with that tantalizing smell, not unlike gasoline and cut grass. It was appetizing but acidic.

I was leaning against a wall wondering what to do. I was thinking about using an ATM machine just around the corner out of sight, when I heard a familiar voice. I stayed still, breathed, listened in.

"Why are you taking out more money?" Mother asked Father. "Didn't you take enough out before we got here?"

"Tracking confusion, Mrs. Macshane," said Mr. Bernard.

"Oh, please, again?"

"Again?"

"The government doesn't care about you."

"Excuse me," Father gasped. "It's their job to care. That's the problem. These are the sorts of actions that will keep their dirty fingers at bay."

"I honestly can't believe you," Mother said. "You don't believe that. You just need to follow your stupid beliefs to their logical ends."

"We've had this argument before, thank you."

"I'm the real atheist amongst us, the reasonable, not argumentative one that—"

"Okay, dear, I get it," Father interrupted.

"Don't 'dear' me. Government is just people. It's not an ATM machine."

"You're saying there's a person in this thing."

"Don't be an idiot," Mother sighed, turning around. Father grabbed his cash and followed behind. "How can you hold both the farthest right and farthest left of all possible political views," Mother continued. "That's why we . . ."

They trailed off. In came two other familiar voices. Bobby and Liana, having waited in line behind my parents, were next to use the money contraption.

" . . . should I take out?" Bobby faded in. "I really want that new cabinet."

"The one in the garage is fine," Liana said. "You don't need a new one, you've had it for years."

"The problem is, I think the kids might have . . ." Bobby lowered his voice, "I think they might have broken into it."

"So they're a little curious."

"No, I don't think you understand."

"I really think Felix and Jessica were expecting us to get something for all of us," Liana said, "not just one of us."

"What? Are you sure?" Bobby asked. "Those two have an age difference that's twice that of Mary and Joseph."

"So? Mary decided to leave home a little earlier, what's your point?"

"Isn't Felix at his age supposed to be narcissistic?" Bobby said. "Don't therapists or psychiatrists or those Internet child experts say self-absorption is inevitable by seventeen?"

"I don't know. What does it matter? You're not getting a cabinet."

"Liana, it isn't healthy nowadays to have a boy not showing a shred of self-centredness. He'll get eaten up."

"Bobby," Liana whispered, "I don't think Jesus died so we could be self-centred."

"Get with the times, my dear. I'm taking enough out to buy me a cabinet, maybe one with a better lock. You?"

"Oh, for heaven's sake," Liana sighed. "Take me out for dinner tonight and I'll look the other way."

I heard beeps, boops, and grunts. The floor clocked with a click as the Clarkson clan scampered away. Someone new sneaked up to the ATM.

" . . . this fucking place," a man faded in. "Why do we come here? I didn't go to Kosovo to protect this sort of democracy."

"Garrett, be calm," another man said. They both sounded young. "It's something to do. And Brad and his partner own a nice little shop here."

"What was wrong with Castro?" the other man asked. "Now there's a place that could prove shopping can have culture."

"Let's not get into that again."

"What do we have here? A talking beaver?"

"Garrett. For God's sake," the other man sighed.

"Don't get me wrong, I love Brad and the J-man and their little soap shop or whatever it is . . ."

"It's a video game store."

" . . . can't we go about it without selling . . ." the man stopped. "Video game store?"

I heard a cash transaction. "Garrett, please be nice."

They walked away. I followed Bobby and Liana a bit until they rendezvoused with Felix. I went my separate way, hoping the my family and the Clarksons wouldn't suffer a chance meet and greet with me in the middle.

I stopped by a used bookstore. It was by far the smallest space in the building, only enough for two cramped aisles. The store seemed like a slab of old Europe. It was almost magical in its ugliness, almost mystical in its claustrophobia. Most of the works were outdated first editions with bland jackets and publishing houses with stuffy names, like William & William. My fractured, fastidiously stuffy European heritage, however, made me feel right at home, as if it and I were genetically intertwined. But what further pushed this place away from my surreal first impressions was the fact that the female barn door that headed this linoleum-floored anomaly seemed to be intellectually well endowed despite an appearance that clearly spelled redneck.

The redneck bookkeeper snapped my attention away from the self-help book case I was blindly digging into. "Looking for something specific there, lad?" she asked. I imagined she was chewing a piece of wheat.

"Not really," I said, overlooking a flamboyantly covered self-help book on self-publishing.

"Well, why not redirect yourself to some better material."

"What?"

"Something that's not interpretative crap."

I put the book back, scanned the shelf. "Why do you stock this stuff then?"

"Are you kidding me?" she said. "It's my most popular section. Do you know how big the industry is, how much work is put into those?"

"Now that you mention it, it is the shiniest section."

"It's damn near huge," she said. "But those are a little too self-centred for me."

"But it's books," I said, confused. "I thought that's what it's about."

"Storytelling is not an individual affair. A book is a lot like life."

"Oh boy," I whispered and looked up. I realized at that moment I couldn't actually see the bookkeeper over the height of the bookshelf. Was I imagining things? Was I even talking to someone?

"In my humble, possibly ignorant opinion, those books are for individualist rednecks," she said.

I possibly was.

"But then again," she continued, "some people might think I'm fresh from Hickville, and that's why I got a degree in literature and bookkeeping."

I was still on the fence.

"Hey, lad, are you like trying to hide from someone, or something?"

No, I definitely wasn't.

I stopped daydreaming, looked out towards the sea of lighted beige seeping into the darkness. Felix, lonely Felix, was heading towards my cramped corner. I ripped out the book I had just put back, turned around, buried my face in instructions on becoming a human spirit-crushing publisher. I had forgotten at that point why I was hiding. With Mother and Father gone I didn't have to worry about it.

I was now hiding for the fun of it.

Felix entered.

"Hey, kid, you didn't answer me," said the bookkeeper.

"What?" I flinched.

"Xavier, what are you doing here?" Felix said.

★

I've fallen asleep again in grump's ruined Jaguar. Felix taps the glass. I roll the window down. "You're a self-centred liar," he says.

"Did you finish it?"

"Not yet, I'm at the mall part."

"You know," I say, still in the car, sticking my head out, "you've insulted me more in the past hour or so than in your entire life."

"So?"

"I thought Christians weren't supposed to swear?"

"Where did you hear that? I'm pretty confident the Bible leaves out the profuse number of times Jesus screams 'mother-fucker' as nails get driven through his hands."

"Right, never thought about that," I say. I step out of the car. "Wait, why are you outside your car? I thought you were pants-wetting scared of forest monsters."

"I saw a spider and it looked at me and I got scared."

"What? Really?"

"Fuck no," he says. "And I'm not afraid of forest monsters either. Prick. I just needed some air. I've been seatbelted to British cow skin for the last couple of hours reading your jack-off novel." He hands me my manuscript.

"Right."

"And speaking of a couple of hours, where the hell is that tow truck," he says. "I thought you said they'd be here sooner."

"I don't fuckin' remember what he said. What time is it?"

"I don't know, I don't have a watch. Check your cellphone."

I pull out my cellphone, flip it open. "It's dead."

"Of course it is."

I click buttons on my phone hoping to see the buzzing start up screen of a resurrection, a return to service and signal strength.

"You know maybe that guy we failed to stop earlier lives around here, and maybe he'd be really kind to us, like most folks are out here, and let us stay at his place until the tow truck came by. We could recharge the cellphone, you could browse his pay-per-view porn selection. It'd be a good night," Felix says.

"I'm good, thank you."

"What? Escort Services?"

"Oh yeah."

"Bullshit."

"What?" I say.

"I don't believe you," he says. "I've known you long enough to know you're not nearly brave enough to do something like that."

"How hard do you think it is to call a classified ad?"

"For you? Impossible," he says. "You wouldn't be able to meet them in a strange room let alone class them up. You couldn't handle it."

I wipe my mouth and look out at the black forest. I rifle through the manuscript pages still in my hands. "What's wrong with this?" I say, lifting up the pages. "You haven't even finished it."

"It's all about you," he says."

"It's an autobiography."

"So?"

"Okay, regardless of what it is, it's about my life, it's supposed to be about me."

"Yeah, but it's just 'I' this and 'I' that," he says. "You know your life isn't just yours. It's other people's too."

"I know that."

"I don't think you do."

"My parents and your family are major characters."

"We're not characters," he says.

I produce a pen, scribble his suggestion on the front page. Felix yanks it back. "Better?" I say. He says nothing, tries to find where he left off. "Why am I liar?"

"What?" he says.

"You called me a liar."

"Well, some of these things," he says, "I don't remember them that way."

"Like what?"

"Like your suicide attempt at that bridge."

"That wasn't a suicide attempt, that was just me thinking."

"I remember a blurb in the newspaper that clearly said: 'Misfit throws shoes at cars before threatening to jump,'" Felix says.

"So I left out one little fact," I say. "That's not lying and you weren't even there. How's the rest of it so far?"

"Have I mentioned I have yet to find a point to this?"

"Fantastic, I've done something right."

Felix melodically stretches his arms, turns his torso, cracks his heals. He walks back to the driver's side and returns to his seat. I stay outside, lean against the passenger door, breathe the air I will surely miss once I return to the city, and stare into the black forest. Felix reads on.

★

"Oh, hey, Felix. I'm just revelling in my own self-absorption," I said, flipping through the self-publishing book.

"What?"

"Nothing. Hey, isn't it Sunday? Why aren't you in church?" I asked.

"I don't know what sort of church you go to, but mine ends at noon," Felix said. "Are you here with someone?"

"What do you think of these self-help books?" I asked. "That bookkeeper thinks they're crap. I just happened to be looking at this one on self-publishing."

"What sort of book would you write?" he asked.

"Now that I think about it, I could probably write something pretty funny," I said. "Like last night my parents got drunk watching

Wheel of Fortune. Again. They drink a lot, then they say things they think are newfound observations, and promise stuff they can't remember. They're probably here buying liquor right now."

"Wow, alcoholism. Yeah, that's hilarious," Felix said, straight-faced. "Is that who you're with?"

"Possibly. No. Why would I be at the mall with my parents? That's just wrong."

"I'm here with my parents," he said. "What's wrong with it?"

"Never mind."

"My dad drinks too. I don't see a problem with it."

"Well, he doesn't seem like it," I said.

"He hides it. He hides it from all of us."

"Then how do you know he drinks?"

"Me and Joseph broke into the cabinet he keeps in the garage," Felix answered. "Three, four shelves of all kinds of liquor and crazy shit. What a stash. We took a bottle of vodka too and he never even noticed."

"Are you sure?"

"Don't tell him any of this, by the way."

"Don't worry, I won't say a thing," I said.

Felix continued, "You think he may be an alcoholic?"

I laughed, loudly. "You think?"

"Well, hell, I don't know," he said. "I've never seen him drunk, at all, and you're the one with the bad parents."

"They're not bad parents," I said. "Okay, well, yes, maybe they are."

"They haven't protected you from themselves."

"Can we stop talking about my parents," I said. "You haven't even met them."

"Do you want me to?" Felix asked.

"No, not really, actually," I answered.

"Hey, lads," the bookkeeper spoke up, "this isn't a lending library."

"It is a bookstore, though, right?" I said.

"Are you going to buy something or not?" she asked.

I looked to Felix. "Do you want this," I asked him, presenting the book.

"No, I already have it." He turned around and left. I put the book back and followed behind. I eyed the Clarkson clan heading in our general direction. "There they are," Felix said, gesturing.

"Is the coast clear?" I asked.

"From what?"

I slid out of the store, feet dragging. I looked to my left. Mother and Father were fast approaching, a weighted bag of alcohol in both of their hands. My veins flowed with irrational annoyance at the very sight, at the thought of a parental meet and greet—a clash between two false religions right in the heart of this heartily fake drywall monstrosity. So I decided to do what most people would: make a sporadic sudden purchase for no particular reason. I beamed it back into the bookstore, the wind whistling with a sudden whoosh as I left the Clarkson clan confused in their spots. Attempting to waste as much time as possible, I grabbed that self-help book on self-publishing, breathing, waiting for Mother and Father to pass by.

They did, eventually. The amount of alcohol they carried was dragging them down.

"No refunds," the pissed off bookkeeper told me.

I walked back to Felix and his happy-go-lucky family.

"What was that about?" Felix asked.

"At the last minute, I decided I wanted that book," I said.

"You told me yesterday you didn't have a job. How could you afford it?"

"I don't," I answered. "But I do have money."

After some chitchat, I left the Clarksons to their Walt Disney-inspired lifestyles and rendezvoused with Mother and Father in the car park. Their emotionless responses led me to believe they hadn't even noticed I had left. Their focus was the beer, the bottles, the high strung instrumental noises they were seeking to hear upon the descent to incoherence, save the security issues with Father's Dodge Omni, which had a sun roof minus the roof part. I began at that point to wonder if Felix was right about my parents.

It was Monday morning. It was a school day. I was heading to school for the sake of tradition. Hordes of the caffeinated loaded in through the front doors in a laborious march fit for a descent into hell. Up near the front was Mr. Tancredo again handing out pamphlets, shoring up support amongst the critical not-legal-age-to-vote demographic. He was a good distance away from being a pensioner. But despite his seemingly out of place existence, he was something of a welcome sight, the same way one feels secure when in the presence of someone far more ridiculous than himself.

"Good morning, Mr. Tancredo," I said.

"Joyous day, my boy, joyous day," he yammered. "Here, take a pamphlet. Some real riveting free literature there for you."

I stopped, snatched a pamphlet. It was a lonely one page, with an obviously outdated portrait of Mr. Tancredo. The entire thing shone with too much gloss. Above his head in bolded Arial text was simply: I'm running for Head Vice Assistant to the Deputy Sanitation Commissioner of Halliburton, Ontario. "I'm the One" was written below his portrait in italics.

"Head Vice Assistant and so on for Halliburton, eh?" I said. "Is that even an elected office?"

"I hope so," Mr. Tancredo answered. "Wikipedia said it was."

"Don't you think you're setting your sights a little high?"

"Look, just tell your parents to vote or something, or you could find out how to turn seventeen within the next couple of weeks," he said.

"Legal age is eighteen."

"Shit, is it?"

"When's voting?"

"I don't know, look it up."

"Mr. Tancredo, I'd be taking this seriously if I actually lived in Halliburton."

"What? Is that what it reads?" He re-read the paper. "Damn those stupid copy centres." Mr. Tancredo chucked his pile of pamphlets into a silver waste bin. "I can't believe they got it wrong."

"How did that happen?"

"Oh, you know, I must have been ranting on about that American company, Halliburton, when they asked for the location," Mr. Tancredo explained. "You know about Dick Cheney?"

"No, should I?" I asked. "Is he Canadian?"

"For God's sake, son, don't you kids know anything about early 90s American politics?" he asked. "Do you know anything about the municipal elections coming up?"

"No, should we?"

"Probably not," he said, buttoning his jacket. "Well, I'm off to find a better copy centre. Luckily those other ones were bought on a huge discount because I use them so much." He began to walk away.

"What should I do with this pamphlet?" I asked.

He stopped, turned. "Have I ever told you the wonders of smoking pot with paper that's made with fifty percent of the ingredients found in children's glue?" Mr. Tancredo asked.

"No."

"I'll tell you about it tomorrow," he said. Mr. Vanman walked to his van and drove off. I held onto the pamphlet, walked into the school.

I coasted through packed hallways, passing shabby lockers, souls, writings, spirits and so forth. I was a sailboat with no sense of direction. I made it to our malnourished library, bumping into Nick at the entrance. At that particular moment, however, he was the one I was looking for as he dependably offered others spare cigarettes. His hair had turned into a dirty dark blonde, and he wouldn't be seen wearing anything but plain shirts and jeans. He had become that fresh-faced handsome fellow waiting for his photograph to appear on teen magazines. Nick's connections within the high school spanned every grade, every social class, every exaggerated insincere categorization people think high school is split into. Nick was one of the few students who managed to retain a job for more than six months so his wealth was gloat-worthy and noticeable. He spent most of it on cigarettes, pot, LSD, and Ecstasy, using it all as leverage to obtain other things. He had gone from trading cards and marbles to THC and MDMA. With his bottomless pockets of shit substances at any-one's disposal, Nick was a main man on campus.

"Hey, shithead," he greeted me. "How's it going?"

"Did you just call me a shithead?" I asked.

"It's a popular greeting in my language."

"Which language is that?"

"The one I made up," Nick said, looking at the paper in my hand. "What's that?"

"It's a political pamphlet," I said. "Mr. Tancredo was handing them out outside."

"Who? What does he want you to do with it?"

"I don't know, roll a joint."

"Man, that would be awesome," he said, jubilant. "You know, I heard those things are made with like the same ingredients found in glue."

"Yeah, apparently so has he."

"Can I have it?"

"Yeah, sure. Actually, no." I brought the pamphlet to my chest. "You're a druggy who comes to school with a broken liver half the time; I'd only be an assistant to your addiction."

"Go start an intervention, see if I care. Besides, it's not my fault."

"Whose fault is it?"

"Parents," he said. "What do you care what I do with it? I'll invite you to another smoking circle."

"You're an idiot," I said. "I ended up lighting a dumpster on fire and nearly burning down the entire school."

"Was that you? That was awesome."

"You tricked me."

"You thought it was a candy."

"You told me it was candy."

"Did I? At least you didn't get caught," he said. "What's done is done. I'll pay you back in cigarettes for your emotional suffering. How much is losing your mind worth?"

"Four packs, with a new lighter."

"Ha, bullshit. I'll give you two and a box of matches," Nick offered.

"Make it three and I'll tell you where there's a pile of these pamphlets."

"Fine." Nick reached into his backpack, counted three packs of cigarettes and a box of matches, threw them to me.

"You carry this much around?" I asked.

"I'm a busy man. Fork over the information."

"The unused silver trash can hidden behind the evergreen tree at the front of the school," I said. "Mr. Tancredo threw away dozens of them."

"See! We are good pals, regardless of . . . something," he smiled, losing his train of thought. He jolted off.

I headed to class.

The smoking circle incident occurred while I was still Grade 12 representative for student council. Nick had invited me behind the school during lunch. It was nothing out of the ordinary. A bit chilly. Snow no thicker than a pizza suffocated the grass of our diamond pitch. The air was muddy, dirty, heavy with a sense of floating claustrophobia. Dark matter had descended from space to our breathing level.

Nick and friends were waiting in a clearing behind the school near a parking lot. The building's dimensions hadn't allowed for a geometrical front and back. It was really just an open space in plain view next to a heating vent. A red dumpster foaming at the mouth with garbage would've been a welcoming splash of colour if it weren't so disgusting. The old stained cardboard boxes around its base—at one time containing fries and fatty foods, frizzy drinks and forgotten gravy—added to the horrible smell. Apparently, happiness is a bottle of coke unless you leave it out in the sun. The large heating vent jutted out of the school's abdomen like an embarrassing tilted dick. It spewed thick steam down to the ground, converting its base into little more than a warm, mucky mud pit. It made the not at all condensed area feel stuffy and enclosed. It provided noise and nothing more, a backdrop of mechanical wheezing.

I casually walked up to the group, nodding, gulping, finishing their half-circle. Nick was to my left, or possibly my right, depending on your narrative perception. He was holding a joint, his hair an absolute mess. His clothes either signalled the life of a committed painter or a man who willingly swam in garbage. Beside Nick was Bryan, the soccer team's star defenseman, a position he contended was under appreciated. "The only advantage," he would say, "is the underrated woman I attract." Bryan was without a doubt still a virgin who believed masturbation counted as sex. He was a nice guy, laconic really, knew exactly what to say at what time and by the age of 16 no less, or sometime around there. At the smoking circle he was dressed for a job interview he was going to after school.

"Why are you here then?" I asked.

"Pot induces confidence," Bryan said. "My last interview was dominated by a scared shitless little man at odds with wanting to be a fuckin' dishwasher."

Beside Bryan was Jesse the drunk, or Jesse the Pigfucker, so named for his love of bacon. A Canadian by birth, American by stereotype, English-Italian by cultural distinction, Jesse was a few pounds overweight and was repeating the 12th grade. He joined the soccer team, played whatever position was assigned to him, and performed with gusto because of his unfounded belief it helped him towards getting a school credit. Jesse, however, was an alcoholic at age 18, showing up to everything at some level of intoxication. "Blame my parents," he would say, when eventually sober. "They kept a fridge stacked shit high with booze."

"And you decided to drink it anyway?"

"They should have known their son was weak kneed."

Jesse was a bit off his rocker holding an open bottle of Jack Daniel's.

Beside Jesse was Bruce, another defenseman. There was nothing eccentric about Bruce. He was polite to the good people, mean to the bad ones, a result of having the most stringent moral compass of any young adult. At the smoking circle that day he wasn't holding anything. Bruce was there to have a chat.

It was something less than a frat party when I arrived. They hollered, chortled in between swigging down slender bottles of tasty concoctions. While Jesse choked down his Jack Daniel's, Nick's mouth was engrossed with the plastic cap of a ginger ale container labelled "Homemade Hard Liquor" in black marker. What a feat of organization on his part, labelling correctly contents that would inevitably beat a few brain cells senseless. At his feet were two tall cans of the cheapest variety. Bryan now had the joint, preparing for his job interview no doubt.

"Well, if it isn't the president of the school," Nick blurted.

"Are you stoned already?" I said.

"Already? I've been at this since the start of lunch."

"Five minutes ago?"

The time of day was a shock to him.

His voice changed volume with every sentence. Nick, whom I had had known in some shape or form beginning in grade three, had degenerated from the quirky athlete I remembered into an unpleasant, wholly insane space cadet. I thought it was a matter of time until he would be expelled from school for blatant stupidity.

"I'm not president of the school," I clarified.

"Sorry, Prime Minister," he said. "My mistake."

"No."

"Governor General?"

"Never mind."

"Chancellor?"

"Shut up."

"Don't tell him to shut up, that's rude," Bryan broke in, straightfaced.

"Oh, I don't care," I said, pulling out a cigarette. "Anyone have a lighter?"

None of them moved, looked, did anything remotely recognizable as human activity. "What's with the smokes?" Jesse asked.

"Is this not an appropriate time?" I said. "Does anyone have a fuckin' lighter?"

"Those are pussy sticks is what they are," Nick broke in, putting down his bottle. Bruce threw me a match box; I nodded. "The only good that comes from them is looking like a cheap fuck and getting cancer," Nick continued. "Now, this stuff is like the real deal. This stuff is meaningful."

Nick had repossessed his joint. He waved it around in my face as if he were clinically blind. The joint had been poorly rolled in orange construction paper. It was taped up with masking tape and burned with an odd colour not found in the rainbow. The scent it produced was just as horrifically indescribable. I coughed, wheezed, attempted to exhale an entire lung.

"I'm fine with my smokes," I said, lighting my cig. It was a breath of fresh air.

They continued passing the joint around. I watched as their pupils grew in dimension. I thought I was watching the universe expand, and as the only one who didn't smoke pot, spatial expansion was all I could think of as an apt description.

Someone was coming, stomping towards us through thin snow. It was a clear day. He was lost in the clarity. The figure was little more than a shadow, a blob, twisting, turning amongst fogged air. Nick and the band of bingers perked up—antelope on the African savannah, had the savannah been served by asphalt parking lots. If they were caught with what they had thieved, they most certainly would be punished, maybe expelled. Their hallucinatory demeanours had shifted to focused stares, transfixed on a non-mystery. I was less afraid of the encroaching object, although being found with the dingbat brigade was an uninviting prospect. I didn't let it get to me. While Nick and his horde had lost all breath, I persisted on enjoying my cigarette.

"What do we do?" Jesse asked, suddenly.

"Shut up," Nick said. "Just, just hide the bottle or something."

"How?"

"Do a fucking magic act for all I care."

Jesse's idea of a magic act was attempting to swallow the still rather full bottle of Jack Daniel's. That quickly turned out to be a bad trick. The poor kid nearly choked to death after the first gulp. He went to plan B. He placed the bottle in the thin snow and attempted to hide it behind his leg. Since Jesse had lost most of his articulation, the bottle not seconds later tipped over, spilling Jack Daniel's guts into the already filthy snow. Jesse had also lost quick reaction time. Not until the bottle had emptied did he realize what he had lost.

"Shit," he said.

He looked down on the spilled beverage as if peering through a glass floor. Nauseatingly, he poked his finger into the white-brown concoction, apparently attempting to pick up the Jack

Daniel's. That didn't work either. He stood up, confused. No one else appeared to have noticed. They were all so amazingly silent.

The figure finally broke through the clarity. It was Jules or Jacque, I can't recall his name. He too was on the soccer team, the much beloved forward known for many assists and generous passing.

"J-man, you idiot," Nick greeted him cheerfully.

"You insult people too much," Jules replied, hands in pockets.

"You scared me."

"What were you scared of?"

"I don't know," he said, taking another puff. "Jesse, God damn it." Nick had noticed the spill.

"It does those things," Jesse replied, absent a mind at that point. "If you wanted some, you should have gotten some yourself, with your money."

"I thought you stole that."

"Did I?"

"This looks like fun," Jules said. "Pass me that orange stick. Did you just get out of art class?"

"I don't know," Nick said, ignoring him. "Jesse, for fuck's sake, you're the only one who's legal age to buy alcohol here, that's why I asked you to get some in the first place."

"Nick it's nineteen, not eighteen," Bruce blurted out.

Nick looked stunned, stoned stunned. "Xavier, could you change that for us?"

"Change what?"

"Legal purchasing age. As president of the school."

"Nick, for fuck's sake."

"Well, whatever you are."

They were disillusioned children, youngsters robbing candy stores of enlightenment. These were friendly folks, the ones I could be found with out on a Sunday morning smoking, talking cheaply the old fashioned way on the church steps with a blind pastor shouting, "God gives me the light to see!" as he fell down slapstick on top of us. But with joints and alcohol in hand, they were the corner store crowd getting high on grass and salted beef jerky.

I was assuming by that point I was no longer conversing with people, but rather with the last remaining wisdom taking refuge in some unaffected section of their brains. I was pretty sure they were a couple of puffs away from departing the twilight zone for a place where they'd discover Jesus in a hamper sipping cocktails, playing the banjo.

"Hey, Alice in Wonderland," Nick called, "do you have any power or what?"

"What?" I sputtered. "Power? No, not really."

"Then why are you president or rep or whatever the hell you're called?"

"I like the title. Looks good on resumes. It's a promoted virtue these days, like eating fast food."

"Why do we have student politics anyway," Jules asked, "if they can't do anything?"

"I don't know. Something fun to do?" I said. "It's sort of like those fucked up tyrannical regimes in Asia or Africa or wherever. These leaders take power and then they name their country the Glorious Democratic Not-At-All Human Abusing Republic of Coca-Cola is Proud to Sponsor Gloraland (registered trademark). It's completely fake, it's complete bullshit, the elections, but it sure looks good on a pamphlet."

"And you want to be a part of it?" Jules asked.

"Can't beat 'em, join 'em."

"But you don't have any power."

"I get discounted cans of pop at the cafeteria," I replied, "and again, if I ever have to brag about it to an employer, I can just lie and say something like, 'oh, yes, I was instrumental in providing greater wheelchair access for the disabled' or something."

Nick laughed. Bruce looked displeased. "Were you?" Bruce asked.

"No, not in the slightest," I said, "but they did require my signature."

"Wow."

"Oh, who the hell cares," I continued. "Nothing will come of it. Our student body president last year, she was the judge of

that stupid Halloween pageant thingy, whoever had the best costume event. Guess who she chose as the winner?"

"Herself."

"Exactly. She said she had the best costume, and she was the
judge. And guess what? The student council agreed or at least
decided not to disagree. It's all just a joke that turns real when
we're all as far away from high school as possible."

"Best years of our lives," Jesse spat. Everyone coughed, snig-
gered with an air of disagreement.

"I don't know a single person who likes high school," Nick
blurted out.

"It's pretty shattering, honestly," Jules added.

"It's fucked up," Bryan said.

There was a silence, but not really since that heating vent was
still spewing noise for no reason. Jesse seemed confused. "Then
where did the phrase come from?" he asked.

We looked around at each other. I passed the joint over to
Jules, disgusted. "Come on, Xavier," Nick said, "take a puff already.
It's great stuff, not the cheap shit; it cost quite a bit."

"I had no idea pot came in degrees of quality."

"Well, let's get you hooked on the good stuff," he said.

I looked to the others. They looked unmoved, dreary-faced
nobodies with a slight stand of superior knowledge, as if realizing that life is fucked from the beginning is a worthy factoid to
brag about to the non-pot-indoctrinated. I let my silence be my
reply.

"Okay, fine," Nick conceded, "but I feel bad that you look to
be the only one here not having fun."

"Where did you get that idea?"

"You don't look happy."

"I never look happy. My regular face just so happens to produce a frown."

"Here, take these," Nick said. In one hand he produced a
globular candy of some sort, and in the other an unopened tall
can.

"What is it?" I asked.

"It's candy."

"It doesn't look like candy," I said, suspicious. "Sort of reminds me of a moth ball. What's that paper looking thingy around its—"

"It'll make you feel better about yourself," he interrupted. "What's not to like?" He took my hand, smacked it into my palm. Then he went wide-eyed when he looked over my shoulder.

"What is it?" I asked.

"Quick," Nick said, "fucking swallow that thing right now and hide this behind your back." He passed me the unopened tall can. He rummaged in his pockets, took out a full packet of cigarettes and passed them out to everyone. "Quickly, take one, everyone, doesn't have to be lighted, just make it look like you're smoking."

"Dude, what the hell?" Jules asked. He looked out into the clarity.

"It's the fucking coach," Nick panicked. "Jesse, for fuck's sake, get rid of that Jack Daniel's bottle, we can't be found with it. Bruce, stomp the joint out, I got more where that came from."

I turned around but didn't swallow the candy. It indeed was the coach, an anal 50-year-old anomaly who appeared from a distance to be a boulder of fat trapped in a picture frame. He was instantly recognizable because of his weight and his love of grey sweaty workout clothes. He appeared to be bending the fabric of reality every time he took a step, an aurora around his figure as the space-time continuum struggled to hold in his bulk.

"If he asks about the cigarettes," Nick continued, "tell him Xavier here gave them to you. He probably doesn't get detentions because he's president." I sneered. "Or whatever, supreme ruler."

"This is stupid," I said. "You guys are on the soccer team. I would think smokes would be a worse thing to be found with."

"No, I see him smoking all the time," Nick said. "He even gets some from me."

"He doesn't appear to be slowing down," Bruce noticed. "He has that look, that huffing rage he has every time the girl's soccer team wins a championship."

"Guys, your pupils are bursting out of your eyes," I said. "You think he ain't going to tell you're all stoned and drunk?"

They didn't answer.

The coach finally made it, breathing regularly. He stared at the six of us, a calm and collected stare on his welcome mat of a face. Nick looked frightened; the rest of them plainly didn't. Then he looked at me. "Who are you?" he bellowed.

"I honestly have no idea," I said.

"I'm Miss California, how do you do?" the coach spat. "What are you doing?"

"Knitting," I coughed.

"Smart ass. All of you got to get back to class; lunch is nearly over," he said, gesturing. None of us moved. "Get going, guys!"

"What for?"

"I'm going to have to remind you guys again how stupid you are."

"Best days of our lives," Jesse said.

"Wait, what's that?" the coach pointed to Nick's feet. Nick had forgotten to hide the other tall can of beer. The vent wheezed and huffed as the six of us looked amongst each other. I clenched the second tall can I had behind my back, rolled my eyes, felt the sting of the chilled air.

"Well?" the coach repeated. "Someone going to answer me?"

"Do you want it?" Nick asked. We glared at Nick. "I don't think we're allowed to have it, if I'm not mistaken. It's still unopened even."

The coach stood pokerfaced, then nodded his head slightly. "How about this," he said. "Give me the tall cans, as well as that pack of cigarettes you're not suppose to be smoking on school property, and I won't kick you guys' asses off the soccer team."

"Fair deal, I would say, eh, boys?" Nick smiled brightly and looked amongst us. We could only return looks of leering annoyance.

"It's your only choice actually," the coach said. He pushed us aside, grabbed the tall cans, the cigarettes, and walked away. "Next time get me a six-pack of Canadian, will you?" he said, his voice fading out.

Nick got back his joint, still lit, secure and burning. "That's how it's done, my friends," he said. "Bribery is a dish best served cold."

"You guys are pathetic," I said. I unfolded my palm still holding the candy and held the remaining tall can in front of me, still not quite sure what to do with either. I took a small swig of the honey-coloured liquid, holding back a cough.

"This isn't the Breakfast Club, Xavier," Nick said. "I mean, look, we have a black kid and an Indian kid too." Bruce and Jules stayed straight faced, staring indignantly. "This isn't some sewing circle," Nick continued, "where we talk and swear at each other about our feelings."

"What do you call it then?"

"We don't call it anything."

I took another swig of the beverage with a fierce upswing of the arm, trying to hide the fact I'd never tasted alcohol before. I looked at my watch. We had to go back to class. I looked inside the circle at the others. Bryan inhaled the last remnants of the joint. He arched his head back and breathed a long stream of smoke out into the crisp ether. His eyes rolled back in his head. He had broken into the gated nirvana I couldn't see or reach. While I watched this, Jesse snatched the glob from my hand, apparently knowing what it was. He took the tall can from me, swigged to wash down the glob, and then calmly returned the can.

"Jess, you idiot, that was for Mr. Cheery here," Nick said.

"That's okay, he can have it," I said, looking around. Bryan was coughing near the heating vent, trying to stay warm as he smoked a cigarette. I took another drink. Then I took another whenever one of them looked over at me.

It went on like this, waiting for a conversation to sneak up on us. Impatient for one to come, Jesse suddenly fell to the ground and began to laugh. It started as a small chuckle. He just chuckled an innocent cackle, his head swinging around digging into the muddy snow. It soon turned into a breathless holler. He held his stomach as if he was out of breath, his "ha-ha" echoing almost sadistically.

"What is his problem?" I asked. I shivered with a nervous twitch.

Jesse just hollered. That's all he seemed capable of. The others looked sullen, confused after exiting their respective tranquilities.

"What's so funny, Jess?" Nick shouted. "Uh? Dude? You can tell us?" He kicked Jesse in the shin lightly and then once in the head, but Jesse didn't stop laughing. He merely squeaked out an "ow" amongst his laughter.

"Do we get someone?" I asked. "He's not stopping."

"Can you guys please shut him up?" Bryan shouted from the vent.

I took a drink from the tall can. I was suddenly hot and sweating.

"Jess, can you please shut up?" Nick said. He stepped over top of Jesse and cupped Jesse's mouth and nose with his hands. "Jess, you're too loud." Jesse squirmed, but he was weak as a leaf. He tried to struggle free. His eyes went wide, then shut, and then opened again looking wet and placid as he struggled for breath. Nick let go and stepped away. Jesse spat, wheezed, coughed, and floundered like a plastered porpoise. He breathed heavily, and then breathed calmer and calmer as he took breath after breath. Jesse relaxed against the perverted earth. It was calm. Then he began to laugh again.

"What a prick," Nick said.

"Why is he doing that?"

"Chill," Nick said. I took another swig. "It must be a side effect or something. Or maybe he just thought of something really funny that he can't get out of his head."

"I was about to eat that glob he swallowed," I choked. "What was it?"

"I don't remember," he said.

A siege of ruined drunkenness lurked amongst the liquid fray of my consciousness. There's actually a surprisingly rational underpinning to being drunk, a mathematical fate to intoxication. By keeping track of the percentage of alcohol one has consumed over time in relation to gender and weight, anyone can calculate a person's blood alcohol content, and in turn know when one more is too much. It's so imperative to know this mathematical buzz kill that bartenders during training must pass knowledge tests rife with drunken horror stories. I took another swig. This was merely experimentation, a combination of chemicals.

My barrier of drunkenness made memories seem like dream sequences driven by intuition and little else. Jesse had fallen asleep on the snow, I'm sure. Bryan, Bruce, and the other guy had disappeared. Nick was a stone statue testing various emotions. In my hand, the tall can was empty and dented. I let it fall to the ground. I felt like I was trying to balance on two feet. Nick was staring at me intently, following the path of my line of sight. His form was boundless, almost transparent, as if the imaginary lines that held his matter together had cracked and overflowed into the space between us.

"What's wrong with you?" Nick asked.

"I'm drunk, I think," I said, "or something."

"Have you ever been drunk before?" he asked.

"If I was, I don't remember."

Jesse squeaked a laugh under his breath.

"What's so funny, Jess?" Nick shouted.

"Forget him. What's wrong with me?" I said.

"There's nothing wrong with you, stop crying," he said. "Why would you think there's something wrong?"

"Look at me!"

"You look fine."

"You're an idiot."

"Are you addicted to booze now?"

"What?"

"Are you?"

"No," I said.

"Then there's nothing wrong with you," he said.

I couldn't say anything more. All I had to do at that point was get back to class. I had this sudden urge to get back to class. The punishment I imagined was severe but unspecific, cloudy with intent. I stumbled away from Nick randomly and in silence. He didn't move, he didn't do anything. He just stayed, standing, staring at me as I left, staring at nothing.

I caressed my hand along the side of the school blind, feeling the precious permanence of every stone and grove, imaging its ingredients, its measure of destructibility. I still assumed measurement was possible in this world. It was a profound assumption, it seemed. I assumed time was ticking away, but didn't peer at my watch, not that my watch would prove anything. I fumbled to the school's front doors, the mechanics of a hinge somehow more difficult to operate then I remembered. There in the empty space, on the unoccupied linoleum, I coasted through the hallways. Peace and quiet amongst a shit storm. I was suddenly enraged, suddenly fuming. The blood was beginning to burn. I suddenly remembered last time in gym class when Nick had thrown a badminton racket at my head in front of everybody. Seeking revenge, on the way out of gym class, I pushed him down a flight of stairs when no one was around. He must have hit his head on the way down because by the time the tumbling stopped, Nick was on the floor not moving. Intuitively, I untied his laces and left him. He didn't remember a thing.

A roar in my hearing was building. I could hear cars, buses, animals, shrieking. That weird leaking aurora effect I had seen on Nick had begun to crop up on the walls. They were like folding, inflatable midway rides, wheezing air out like a balloon. I was stumbling about, babbling pointless language, mumbling insults at Nick. Things seemed wavier than usual. Soon crowds of people descended before my corrupted vision, and I was surrounded, alone, in a crowded hallway. I stood still, eyes cocked up inside my head, detailing every invisible note of the murmurs that passed by my ear. It was tranquility inside pure chaos. In this world, I had unknowingly lit a cigarette—that spine tingling whoosh sound of flames finding paper to eat. I was becoming forgetful of my place in space. I thought I was invisible, transparent, a ghost. People were getting to me. I pushed them, tripped them, called them names. I shoved my way back the way I came and went to that red dumpster near the smoking circle.

Popcorn butterflies fizzing and curdling in flames. Popcorn butterflies folding in on themselves until shrivelled husks. Drops of butter fly from fresh popcorn and land on human flesh. Something about chemical composition makes dried butter flammable. Something about the world makes it disposed to burning.

Nick had almost done it before; maybe he could take the fall if it did.

I stabbed at my pockets and pulled out the match box I'd borrowed from Bruce. I lit the entire thing aflame and threw it into the dumpster. I didn't stay and watch to see flames swallow garbage or attempt to navigate towards bigger prey. I threw the flaming matchbox into the dumpster's mouth and ran home.

★

The pages have stopped turning. The manuscript is an organized tangle across the lap. A midnight wind leaks into the Jaguar's open car window and pushes pages about like empty beer cans. I am back in the ruined blue Jaguar beside Felix in the driver's seat. He has fallen asleep.

I exit the exquisite mess, push my feet into the gravel shoulder. I get goosebumps from that sound, that sound of moist stones ruffling and scratching against each other, avalanching down a small hill made up of ever more moist stones. I pelt the forest with the highway pebbles, the remnants of rock blasting and bulldozing. I assassinate maple leaves, blitzkrieg pine trees, mortar fallen oaks, litter the forest's footing with pale blue pebbles.

I saunter up and down the highway shoulder looking for perfect stones. I love what I'm finding deep in the ditch instead. A broken stopwatch. A sandwich container. A pipe (someone's muffler?). Some glass. Some glasses. An empty purse that smells of alcohol. The temperature is chilly. I dig into my jean pockets and retrieve my matchbox. I throw the purse up the slight embankment, encircle it in stones, and light it ablaze. It whooshes, it cackles, a makeshift camp fire. I walk over and take back my manuscript from sleeping Felix. I review the pages. He has fallen asleep while reading of my miniature drunken rampage (happy dreams).

Who, I think, would want to read about my life? I am a faceless face to everyone else as much as they are to me. They have their own ruined lives to deal with, their own weaknesses to reconcile, their own strengths to utilize, their own problems with people and reality and talking and so forth. What can I possibly offer with mine?

I look through the pages once more. By memory I mark all the places where I told the truth. I rip out those marked pages with surgical precision and throw them into the fire. It is hard to believe just how much truth I have mistakenly put into this manuscript of mine. Purely accidental.

Felix awakes to the screams of purse leather losing its pretentiousness. With no sense of urgency, he lumbers over to my fire pit. "I mean to be an asshole in every way when I say the proper place for that story is in this fire," he says.

I say nothing, find another page of truth, throw it in.

"What are you doing?" he says, his voice like gravel. "Burn the entire thing. Start over."

"When Nabokov was writing *Lolita* he nearly threw his unfinished manuscript into the fire," I say. "But he didn't because he was afraid it would come back to haunt him."

"Or he got distracted by a butterfly."

"I think I'll make this into a work of fiction that's based off lies influenced by a life lived in denial and confusion," I say.

"Why lies?" Felix asks.

"Because everyone always attempts to be right; everyone thinks they're right," I say. "So I will be the first human being in history, I'm presuming, to actually hold beliefs I know are wrong and will say are wrong but won't give up."

"What are you burning?"

"Someone's purse."

Felix looks into the fire. "You are one hell of an angry individual."

"You told me that a couple of hours ago."

"I remember that dumpster fire," he says. "I remember all those rumours of pushing people down stairs, those student speeches you held, the destruction."

"And?"

"Why, why did you do that? What satisfaction could it have provided? I mean you're still an angry person today even after all that. No wonder people like you, the un-spiritual, tend to sound and feel robotic to me."

"I'm spiritual."

"You're babbling."

"I'm very connected with myself and the universe that I see."

"A very bleak and violent universe, it must be."

"Same old, same old," I say.

"Did you ever think you were actually going to go through with it and stab Nick?" he says.

"Maybe. I'll never know. I already threw that page into the fire."

Headlights shine on the inadequate blue beams of steel on wheels, the murderous protruding arm of a tow truck painting itself in the darkness. The thing clunks to a halt. We walk over, leaving the fire to burn.

Data is filed, huffs are exchanged, the plain named Carl of Oakville or Orangeville or Oshawa or somewhere in that region mates the arm with the rather evil looking blue Jaguar. Bubble gum is chewed, wheels are lifted from the pavement, and bodies are squished into the three seater tow truck.

We drive off. The purse fire gleams in the rearview mirror until it is out of view. Felix has fallen asleep again and Carl is laconic.

"So, Carl," I ask, "why aren't you named Bulldog or Gravedigger like the rest of those guys?"

"It's just a name," he says.

I'm asleep in the cab when I'm awoken by a thud from the glove box. I feel my coat lining to make sure my deformed man-uscript is still rolled up in my pocket. The paper pokes out obtru-sively. Carl is already unseated, hoisting down the Jaguar, and Felix is just stepping out. I rub my eyes. They feel like glass. The tow truck jerks again and the Jaguar is returned to its four wheels. I open up the glove box to investigate the disturbance. An unloaded pistol.

It didn't take long to get back to Toronto. It's still dark and there's no chance of a sunrise yet. The tow truck lot is fairly north of the city proper and sits on an optical illusion: it looks like we're parked on a plateau, hundreds of metres above sea level, but we're not. It's just the flat landscape swooping towards Lake Ontario.

Looking south, low-rise housing grows from every patch. The once lush, fertile Ontario farmland has been replaced by tile, roof gravel, and mechanical apartment boxes. Nonetheless, I can see a cacophony of lights shining from downtown. Blood red and snow white arteries squirm towards the business district. Airplanes drown out whatever you have to say on their way to Pearson International. The highway blares like it's above my ears. I've been to the Atlantic Ocean. This highway sounds a lot like an ocean's tide.

I'm still in the tow truck cab. I feel underneath the seat, feel the floor, investigate the glove box. I'm looking forlornly for ammo.

Carl returns and gestures for me to get out. Felix reviews his Jaguar again. The car lot is a no-man's-land of the previous night's drunk driving circus. Empty tow trucks randomly rest around a cubed office. Every now and then a driver will step into the outhouse-like office, silhouette in the window for a few minutes, and then leave with a paper cup of coffee. Overalls, baseball caps, dirty pens, dirty paperwork, steel-toed boots. The drivers' rugged hands miss one thing. I head to the parked tow trucks and notice that each one is unlocked and ready to load, keys welded to the ignition. I search every glove box of every tow truck in hopes of finding the bounty. Most have shotguns, three have mace, two have pistols, but only one has a loaded, concealable firearm. I steal that one, pocket the contraption in my pants. It presses against my torso, my belt doing double duty.

I call a cab before Felix's car is ready. I tell him I'll meet him later in the day. I go home and rest for a bit, waiting for a sign of the sun. I go to my mother's. My mother is awake when I arrive, or I woke her upon my arrival. She swings the door open, drearily. Neither of us is good at greetings.

"I decided to come uninvited," I say.

"I would never have guessed. I haven't seen you in forever," she says.

"Can I use your balcony?"

"That's your hello?" she says. "We've only heard each other's voices through a phone for God knows how many months and now you want to use my balcony?" She rubs her eyes.

"Can I?"

"It's already in use, being attached to the building and all."

"I don't plan on taking it with me."

"Just come inside, please," she says, stepping out of the doorway. "If you need a place to stay, food, water. Not drugs. I don't have any left. Aspirin. Do you need Aspirin? What am I saying? Your liver is probably made of aspirin at this point. Coffee? Actually, no. If you're looking for coffee, you'll have to go back downstairs."

I peer around her apartment. It looks like she has yet to fully unpack her belongings nearly a decade into her condo ownership. "You know, in our society, it's customary to unpack your boxes once you've moved in," I say.

"I'll kick you right back out, too early for your sense of humour," she says. "That was humour, wasn't it?"

"Yes."

"It's awful, get a new one."

"When did you become my old Jewish grandmother?"

"Oh lighten up," she says. "You never had a Jewish grandmother."

"Position's open," I say.

"Actually, you never met your grandmother on my side did you?" mother asks.

"That's right, I didn't. How was she?"

"You didn't miss much."

"I would have liked to meet her," I say.

"You would have liked to make fun of her," Mother says. "I know you well enough to know you wouldn't have liked to meet her."

"What's that suppose to mean?"

"You would have wanted to meet a new character," she says, "I doubt you would've been polite enough to sit through some Irish Catholic persecutory delusion bullshit."

"It's weird to think I'm part Irish," I say, sitting down on a groovy plastic chair. "It doesn't feel that way."

"How is being Irish suppose to feel?" she says.

"I don't know, different then the feeling of being French," I say.

"How does it feel to be French?"

"I don't know, it doesn't feel like I'm that either."

"You didn't really get a chance to not get along with your father's family."

"It's like I was adopted," I say.

"You definitely were not," she says. "Don't deny the recognition I deserve for carrying your proto-little-self in my stomach."

Mother flops onto her couch. Her hair is black and greasy and drapes the couch's headrest like wet curtains. I step out onto the balcony. The sky is a challenge to find. I'm surrounded by panel glass from equally tall office towers and condominiums a mere street's width away. I produce the black pistol. My knowledge of firearms is limited to movies I recall having watched. I check the cartridge, the safety, the shiny steel that forms a metallic banana. I take my manuscript from my pocket and unroll the dirty, damp pages. I look over the object. I caress its threadlike quality, its sandpaper surface, its roughed exterior. The manuscript's weight is a weird feeling, I forgot how bloated it became. I forgot how flammable paper feels.

I raise the pistol to my line of sight, look through the tiny iron gate attached atop the tube and point it at a neighbour's balcony protruding from the condo next door. A wonderful weighted feeling. I'm less interested in its effects than its physics. I point the gun in various directions, never taking my sight away from the iron sights. There are no people down below for me to pretend to shoot, no victims for my sniper fantasy.

Mother heaves the balcony door open behind me.

The contraption jumps in my hands, falls over the balcony's edge, drops to the pavement below. I am somewhere above the 15th precipice. The gun hits the ground with a crack.

"Are you drunk?" Mother asks.

Felix's Jaguar is fixed. Whatever ailed the middleaged automotive is gone, cured thanks to a magician mechanic who suggested putting gas in the tank. Felix pays a tow truck fee, a fee that protected him from having to walk down a highway at night to retrieve fuel. Felix's mulish pride is unscathed. He drives back home and rests for a couple of hours before waking up close to dawn. He can't sleep. It's not that his girlfriend is not a live-in girlfriend yet. It's something else.

Felix descends back to the parking garage and re-seats himself in his Jaguar. The sun is out, barely. He drives in perfect squares around the city's grid plan for a few minutes before heading to my father's awful photography office. It's just opening up for a day's worth of uncanny and deprived passport photos, chestnut wedding portraits, troubling Student I.D. cards, red-eyed camping trips, black and white picture frames, people that don't understand photo capture technology, Father's atheist one-liners.

"Hello, sir, can I help you?" Father greets Felix from behind the unimaginative reception desk.

"Will, it's me," Felix says. "It's Felix."

"Felix? I don't remember you, but I can see if your prints are in or not," Father says. "Were you the one with the weird wedding or the high school administrator that liked to crack jokes about how ugly the students were this year?"

"Neither."

"Who are you again?"

"Will, we've met before. I'm Xavier's friend," Felix says.

"The Christian one?"

"Sure."

"Can't say I really remember you very well," Father says. "What's Xavier up to these days anyways? Keeping busy?"

"I would think that'd be a question I should be asking you."

"You'd think," Father says. "He hasn't been talking much lately."

"Did he talk to you about his autobiography?" Felix says.

"Autobiography? About who?"

"Santa Claus. Himself, of course."

"Why would he do that?"

"I don't know, it's worrying. His life isn't even that interesting."

"You came here to tell me that?"

"No."

"Are you here to see our specials on frames?" Father asks. "We *are* having a twenty percent off sale, although you might have to buy rejected portrait photos to get the discount. I can double check."

"Fuck's sake," Felix says. "I think Xavier's going to do something. Something harmful. Possibly to others, most likely to himself."

"I doubt that. He's always been very well behaved and considerate."

"He tried to set our high school on fire."

"Today?"

"No!" Felix says. "Will, I need you to help me here. I think Xavier is going to do something criminal."

"Let the jails take care of it. My taxes already pay for those anyways."

"And if he kills himself doing it?"

"Then I suppose he won't go to jail."

"Um . . ."

"You're paranoid," Father says. "Xavier has no history like that. What could possibly lead a frightened, cynically humourless kid his age to do the stuff you apparently think he's capable of?"

"I have a hunch. Why aren't you taking this seriously?"

"For starters, you've just come into my photography store at an ungodly hour to talk about a version of Xavier I never met."

"Did Xavier call you a bad father?"

"I don't really want to talk about that with you," Father says. "What do you want me to do? You worry he'll do something wrong? You want me to call him?"

"That could help."

"What gave you the impression he would do something bad?"

"When we were at the tow truck lot, I saw him snooping around in other people's tow trucks."

"Why were you in a tow truck lot?"

"That's not important. What if he stole a weapon or something?"

"Why would he do that?"

"I don't know, revenge?" Felix says. "I came to you to see if you could provide insight on your son."

"You've come to the wrong place."

"Well, where should I have gone then? Aren't you worried?"

"Excuse me, Felix," Father says. "Let me repeat: you just came into my store and started talking about an Xavier I never met. How do you expect me to understand what you are talking about?"

I step back into the porch, sit down on the couch, and fold my manuscript back into my coat pocket. Mother hands me a glass of water and sits beside me. "Have you found a girlfriend yet?"

I roll my eyes. "Oh, you know women, they just come and go," I say. "Matter of fact, I burned through six or so just last month."

"Sure you did," she says.

"Honestly, I did. I'm cool that way," I say.

"You need to fall in love."

"Definitely not."

Mother sighs loudly. "Why did you come to me today for support? You told me and your dad a long time ago that we were bad parents."

"I didn't say I needed support."

She leans across the space between us and hugs me, kisses me on the cheek. "I'm a bad parent," she says, "I admit it, but I'm not a bad human being."

"For the love of God," I shift in my seat, suddenly uncomfortable. "Why do you have to be so motherly?"

She folds back to her side of the couch. "Did you drop something over the edge of the balcony?"

"No I did not."

"I thought I saw something fall."

"Optical illusion. I was pretending to shoot out office windows and sniper people with my finger gun."

"You're a little old for that," shy says. "Why did you come here then? Not that I'm complaining, I'm glad you're here. But you can understand how your behaviour is a little suspicious."

"I just wanted to say hello. Can't a son say hello to his mother, uninvited?" I say.

"At this early hour?"

"I couldn't sleep. And I just came from a tow truck lot."

"A tow truck lot?"

"Felix's car got towed."

"You guys got in a car accident?" she asks.

"It's not important."

"Are you okay?" Mother says. "You weren't planning to jump off my balcony, were you?"

"What? Why would you say a thing like that?"

"Suicide tends to run in the family."

"I haven't met much of my family so I wouldn't know," I say.

"Well those that did commit would be dead anyways."

"Wait, did either you or Dad ever make an attempt?" I ask.

"This isn't the time to talk about it, Xavier."

"It's the perfect time. I mean, look at the weather. It's beautiful."

"I think you need to rest," she says.

"It's been an odd couple of hours," Felix says, wallowing in the photography office, "and I can assure you, something is up with Xavier."

"You should have gone to his mother's then," Father says.

"Is that where he is?"

"I don't know, did he tell you where he was going?"

"No," Felix says.

"Then he's at his mother's," Father says.

"Well then," Felix says, joyous. "Let's fucking go!"

"Why?"

"To help him. Or something."

"I don't know what's going through your mind right now," Father says, "but your sense of urgency seems misplaced. Now, I am not some unemotional blob. I do give a shit about my son. But when you become a father, you'll understand the role playing a father has to fit into."

"You're a misanthrope, I got it," Felix says.

"Like hell I am."

"If Xavier wanted to hurt someone, who would that be? Let me put it that way."

"What are you talking about?"

"I wouldn't be bringing it up if I wasn't concerned," Felix says.

"It definitely would be more than one person with him," Father says.

"I was a little sleepy at the time, but I'm pretty sure he admitted to me that he wanted to hurt someone," Felix says.

"You think he said that?"

"I know he said that."

Father walks around the front desk. "Okay," he says. "Hey, Roxanne," father shouts, "I'll be back in five minutes." He turns to Felix. "If you think it's important. I need more printer ink anyway. Can we stop by an Office Depot first?"

I hug Mother goodbye and tell her I need some fresh air and a better view. It's still rather deserted outside. I walk around her building trying to triangulate what space her balcony overlooks. I recon the pallets of concrete that surround the vicinity of her side of the building. Burned cigarette butts, waterlogged garbage, crushed stones, footprints, alcoves of gum, a dirty and dented little black pistol. The pistol had bounced its way into a flower bed. I pocket the pistol and stop at a phone booth. A crumpled phone book page with Nick's work address ruffles loudly in my coat pocket.

My heart is thumping. I'm sweating in rather chilly weather. I wipe my sweaty hands on my manuscript. I take it like a towel, pat my hands on the front page a couple of times, then stuff it back into my coat pocket.

Nick is head honcho at a fast food chain. The fast food chain is a huge corporation, so the chain's façade is replicated dozens of times over all across the city. Nick has been head honcho at this fast food chain for quite a while. Nick bakes pot into his restaurant's brownies. Nick is the same Nick I've known for so long.

I walk around to the back of Nick's restaurant and reach a service entrance. A lanky kid in a black apron sits on a plastic milk crate and smokes a cigarette. He leans back against the brick wall of the building. To his right is the brown door of the service entrance and to his left is an open green dumpster. The branded baseball cap he's required to wear is reversed on his head. Greasy black hair pokes from beneath its rim. I ask him if a guy named Nick is around. He opens the service entrance door and yells for Nick. The lanky kid continues to smoke his cigarette, stares down at his shoes looking for dirt and inconsistencies. Nick steps out, wipes his hands on a cloth, drapes the cloth across his left shoulder. "Xavier?" he says.

"That's me," I say.

"How you've been?" he asks. "You're looking good."

"You look well-marbled."

"It's the deep-fryer," he says. "Cheap tanning if you spend enough hours in front of one. What are you doing here?"

"I'm looking for a free meal," I say. He laughs. "I was just in the neighbourhood." The lanky kid finally finishes his cigarette and goes back inside. I wait for the door to shut. I wait for that rush of air and that loud clunk of a steel door—the ultimate sound of denial. "I was in the neighbourhood, thought I'd drop by to see if you remember me."

"It's only been a couple of months since we last hung out," he says. "I hope you still smoke, not because I want you to get cancer, but because right now I need a cigarette."

"By all means," I say. I reach into my coat pocket. I can feel the cold metal of the gun. My hand brushes across its unforgiving surface as I grasp my matchbox. I toss Nick the matchbox and he gestures a thankful salute.

"Been doing any drugs lately?" he smiles.

"No," I say, earnestly.

"Lighten up, it's a joke. You like jokes?" he says. "I can definitely hook you up with some stuff if you need it." Nick lights his cigarette, waves out the match, throws the sizzling stick into the dumpster. "I feel like we've spent most of our time together out back beside dumpsters."

"Trying to light them on fire."

"Making mistakes, you should say. We never intended to and luckily we never did," Nick says. "I'm no vandal."

"Thinking back, though, I would say you were a bit of a bully," I say.

Nick shrugs his shoulders, takes an extra long drag on his cigarette. He chuckles lightly. "You're breaking my balls," he says. "You seem a little uptight. When's the last time you got laid?"

I don't smile or say anything. I attempt to communicate to Nick that I won't answer that question through a stern facial expression.

"I don't know what to say to an accusation like that," he says. "Shoot me."

I slip my hand in my pocket and wrap my palm around the gun's rough handle, a façade of meaningless spotted brail ensuring my sweaty flesh doesn't slip its grip.

"Is something wrong?" Nick asks.

"People keep saying that. Do I look sick?" I say.

"You look like you're on a mission."

"Let's get back to how you were a bully," I say.

"I gotta go back to work here soon, let's talk about it later at the pub," Nick says. "You know a friend of mine, whenever he had a bad break-up, would invite his ex out for drinks shortly afterwards, like that same week. He'd get shitfaced, apologize profusely in between pints, and then remember nothing the next morning."

"That's your plan?"

"It's a good plan," Nick says. I shake my head. "Dude, what do you want me to say? You want me to apologize? You want me to say sorry for calling you names? I never pushed you around. I was never violent."

"Your attitude stunk."

"Who cares?" he says. "You're being pretty weird coming here before we've even finished reheating yesterday's scrambled eggs, talking about childhood shindigs. I'm not saying sorry, and I don't want to get into any of this 'I was just a kid' bullshit either. Just toughen up."

I clench the pistol tightly and pull it out of my pocket. The handle is warm and wet. My trembling hand raises the barrel to my eye's line of sight and points it straight at Nick. He smirks.

"You've brought a toy gun to a knife fight," he says.

"Humbert Humbert shoots Claire Quitly. George Milton shoots Lennie Small. Tyler Durden shoots himself. Barney Panofsky can't remember if he shot Boogie. Several people try to shoot Yossarian. Lewis Miner fails to prevent his principal from getting shot," I say, "and now Xavier shoots Nick."

"Just one shot. I heard pellet guns can break the skin at close range," Nick says.

"It's not a toy gun."

"Yes it is."

"No, it's not. Listen to me."

"I'm listening, go ahead," Nick says.

My hand squirms around the gun's handle. I shift my feet and try to stare down my opponent. My coat suddenly feels heavy and excessive. "I don't actually have anything to say," I say. "But it's not a toy gun."

"Yes it is," he repeats. "You know how I know?"

"How?"

"Because you're no vandal," he says. "You don't have the capacity to harm someone. You're too afraid of people."

"That doesn't make any sense."

"I've known you since grade school," he continues, "I know these things. I'm just the sort of bloke whose observations you should heed." Nick smiles, stomps on his cigarette.

"You're ruining the atmosphere," I say. I place my index finger on the gun's trigger. I want to finish the final muscular activity required to operate the metal contraption to its fullest potential. I am ready to prove Nick wrong.

"Hold that thought," Nick says. He gestures for me to hold off. I can hear his noise sniffling, breathing in and breathing out. "You smell that?"

"I smell your demise," I say.

"Well we must be smelling two different things, because I smell burning garbage," he says. He looks over at the dumpster. Small orange waves rise from the open lid. "Fuck," he says. "Let's reschedule." He smiles at me, bobs his head, and then bolts into the service entrance. He comes back out with a bucket of water and another lanky kid wearing a black apron and clutching a phone. I quickly shove the gun back into my pocket. The fire department and police are going to be coming soon judging by Nick's ineffective bucket of water.

More of Nick's employees are coming to investigate, running back and forth from the service entrance, unsure what to do. I kick at stones and observe my surroundings. I count milks crates, neighbouring fast food chains and apartment buildings. I lurch around the lot for a bit, looking back to see if Nick has registered by diminishing presence. I finally walk far enough away that I can no longer hear the wailing anxiety of a fire truck.

There's a centuries old bridge close to the city centre that overlooks a lush ravine. It's a multi-dimensional ravine. Highways, bicycle paths, running water, and wildlife share the same snaking depression, the same line in the sand that cuts the city's grid plan in two. I'm geographically in between two halves when I reach the bridge's midpoint.

The bridge exudes a stony nostalgia of Whitey McConcrete, Slanty McGee, and Immigrant Haus all rolled into one. It's a suspicious nostalgia of home. The low, thick bridge rail makes it seem more like a cliff's edge than a bridge filling its potential by traversing a gulf between two topographical slices. I climb onto the stone ledge and sit down, feet dangling over the ravine. Below I can see the plethora: a soccer field, two roadways, bike path, railroad tracks, forest, a slow river of cloudy water. The still rising sun shines brightly. The sun is pointing a gun of light rays and radiation directly at my being.

Is there an unmerited sequel in my future?

I pull the gun out of my pocket and study the shape, the shadow it casts on my lap. I look down at the blur of green vegetation several metres below and then back at the gun. What do I do with it? Perhaps I should keep it for a rainy day when Nick seems more shootable, more disposed to populating his stomach with bullets. I vigorously wipe clean the sweaty gun handle. I place it precariously on my lap and unfurl my equally sweaty and stained manuscript. The paper, though, will not wash clean with the same sort of wipe down as the gun. A breeze pushes at my back. The gun begins to slip off my lap. I clasp it tight in my hand.

Someone shouts my name. I'm startled. I shove the gun quickly into my coat pocket and try to hold onto the pages of my manuscript at the same time. I manage to get hold of the first page but the weight of the hundreds of others pulls the first one loose. The bundle of paper, still clipped together, slips between my legs and falls. It furls and ripples on its way down.

I look around, but I'm blinded by the sun. I keep my balance and swivel my head. I hear my name again, shade my arms. "What do you say in a situation like this?" the person asks.

"You found me," I say.

Acknowledgements

I want to thank all the people who took the time to read versions of the manuscript and helped me shape the story into what it became.